I0702366

A Bent Creek Christmas

A Harker Brothers Ranch Prequel Novella

Catie Cahill

All rights reserved. No part of this publication may be reproduced, distributed, or transmitted in any form or by any means, including photocopying, recording, or other electronic or mechanical methods, without the prior written permission of the author, except in the case of brief quotations embodied in critical reviews and certain other noncommercial uses permitted by copyright law. For permission requests, write to the author at:

http://www.catiecahill.com

This is a work of fiction. Names, characters, businesses, places, events, locales, and incidents are either the products of the author's imagination or used in a fictitious manner. Any resemblance to actual persons, living or dead, or actual events is purely coincidental.

Copyright © 2022 Catie Cahill

Cover design by Erin Dameron-Hill, EDH Graphics

Contents

Come home to Bent Creek

A small town in Montana where everyone knows everyone, secrets live in the shadows of the mountains, and love is just waiting to be found. One by one, the Harker brothers return home to reclaim their ranch, face their family's past troubles with the Nobles, and find the love they didn't know they needed.

Chapter One

Marybeth

October

The letter was impossible.

And yet there it was in black and white, an offer to buy the building that housed my shop for a ridiculous amount of money.

I skimmed to the end. It was from a large development firm with a Chicago address. Some place miles and miles from Bent Creek, Montana, with the signature of someone I was sure had never even stepped foot into my small town.

I refolded the letter and shoved it onto a messy shelf under the cash register, one that held a barrage of broken ornaments, torn Christmas cards, and discarded receipts. Why I was keeping it, I didn't know. Selling this place was something I'd *never* do, not for anything.

But I'd be lying if I said that amount of money wasn't tempting, especially right now.

"Maybet!" The sound of a sweet, squeaky voice pulled me from my thoughts. I smiled when I saw Diego's adorable, sticky face peering up at me from below the other side of the counter.

I pretended to study him seriously as I leaned over the counter. "You had peanut butter for lunch, didn't you?"

His big brown eyes widened. "You know, Maybet!"

I nodded, serious as sin. Then I tapped my temple and said, "I know everything."

Diego looked behind him to his mother—and my best friend. Larkin Reyes grinned and shrugged her shoulders.

Diego glanced back at me. The telltale swipe of peanut butter under his lower lip gave everything away. I reached below the counter and pulled out the Rubik's Cube that some tourist had left behind, and that I kept just for Diego. I held it out to him, and his chubby hands grabbed it on either side.

He toddled over to the corner between two sets of shelving and plopped down, twisting and pulling at the Rubik's Cube. He had no idea what it was or what the point of the puzzle was; he just loved turning the different colors and admiring the patterns he created.

Diego satisfied for a few minutes, I stepped out from behind the counter to hug my friend. Larkin looked exhausted, but that seemed to be her permanent state ever since Diego was born. Raising a baby on her own and scraping by to make ends meet would do that to anyone.

She chewed on her lip now, her attention on Diego in the corner.

"What's wrong?" I asked. She looked more stressed out than usual today.

She shook her head. "Nothing more than the usual. Mom got called into work, and Mrs. Hopkins's mother is in the hospital."

I held up a hand. "Leave him with me. He can help me close up and you can pick him up at the ranch when the coffee shop closes."

Larkin turned to me, her brown eyes—exact replicas of Diego's—soft with gratefulness. "Are you sure? If a bunch of customers come in, you're not going to want a toddler running around underfoot."

I spread out my arms. "I think all these customers can handle it." It was meant to be a joke, but the bitterness seeped through.

"It'll get better, Marybeth," Larkin said, grabbing one of my hands and squeezing it. "The tourists will come flocking in. They always do."

I forced myself to smile, but what I couldn't say out loud—because I could barely admit it in my head—is that I was afraid this year wouldn't be like the others.

That the bills to keep this place open would become too much. That I'd *have* to sell or declare bankruptcy. That I'd have to live the rest of my life on the ranch with my brother.

I took a deep breath, forced the smile even more because Larkin had enough on her mind without hearing my worries too, reassured her Diego would be fine, and shooed her out the door to her job.

Leaning against the doorframe, my gaze flitted between Diego in the corner and Larkin walking half a block down to the coffee shop in the couple inches of snow that had fallen overnight. And I wondered if I shouldn't just let the inevitable happen.

Opening a Christmas shop in Bent Creek was a novelty, but something I'd fully believed in. My brother Luke thought I was crazy when sweet old Mrs. Caldwell left me this corner building in her will and instead of selling it, I decided to open my shop. And it went well, for a couple of years.

Bent Creek wasn't a destination itself, but it was a cute, old town with a stunning mountain backdrop, located smack in between two popular ski resorts. When people got tired of the pretend, manufactured old-timey shops and restaurants in the ski resort towns, they came here for the real thing.

But this last year had been different. The tourists still came, just not as many of them. And I'd noticed it in summer too, when the resorts were quieter, but the budget tourists came to enjoy hiking and mountain climbing and white water rafting. They'd stayed in the resort towns. Then fall arrived and the tourists kept staying away from Bent Creek. The skiing was due to start soon, and then I'd know for sure.

Sam Watson, who ran the soda and ice cream shop across Main Street from me, said it was because of the big development companies pouring money into those resort towns. They kept building and growing and there was no reason for anyone to leave to come here. The mayor said they'd get tired of it soon enough and come back. But we hadn't seen it happen yet.

I blew out air, which sent my bangs flying up from my face as I crossed my arms against the October chill. Larkin disappeared into Mountain Roasters minutes ago, and yet I still couldn't seem to leave my post in the doorway. The streets weren't completely empty, but I knew most of the people I could see from here. There were a handful of obvious tourists, but a handful wasn't going to keep Bent Creek Christmas open.

Are you crazy? Sell it. Luke's words from back when I came up with the idea for the shop echoed in my head. Maybe I should have done just that. But I loved this place. I couldn't imagine not coming here every day.

I slipped back inside my empty store, wove around my displays and decorated Christmas trees, and offered Diego some crayons and paper, and retreated behind the counter. That envelope caught my eye again.

It would be so easy. Sell it before the debt accumulated too much, take what would be left, and . . . do what? Leave?

My heart constricted at the thought. Leaving might've been easy for my other brothers and my parents, but it wouldn't be for me. But if I sold this place and stayed, I'd have nothing.

There was the ranch, but that was more Luke's than mine, now that he was okay most days. I didn't have a college degree. No useful skills other than riding horses and making small talk with customers. No boyfriend. No impressive work history. No apartment. No nothing.

All I had was this shop and this town. Larkin and Diego. Luke, who needed me less and less as time went on.

Diego must have known something was bothering me because he abandoned his crayons, waddled over, and wrapped his sweet arms around my jeans-clad leg. I reached down and rubbed his back.

Giving up felt like betraying everything and everyone that meant something to me. And I wouldn't do that. I *couldn't*.

I'd fight for Bent Creek and the people I loved until I took my last breath. And that meant fighting to keep this shop going.

No matter what.

Chapter Two

Gabe

December

It was the sign that almost did me in. Almost made me spin around in my rental Ford F-150 and run right back to the airport and Chicago.

How was the *same* sign still there? That blue and white *Welcome to Bent Creek* with the snow grazing the top, the mountain background, and bullet hole nicking out the bottom left corner that Nick put there senior year. The memory burst open, and I gripped the steering wheel. Everything was falling apart that night, and Nick and I found ourselves with one too many beers and one of Pops's pistols.

It was one of the last good memories I had with my brother, if you can call it *good*. I don't even remember the last time we talked.

I forced myself to keep driving past that sign.

I took the long way so I didn't have to drive by Quarter Mile Road. If I didn't see it, maybe I could act like the ranch never existed. Like my memories were some kind of fabrication, or like I was in some other town altogether.

There never was much to Bent Creek, and that hadn't changed. Some of the houses I passed were painted different, a few trees were gone and others had grown. A couple of businesses on the edges of town were new. But really, it was the same place. Snow-covered, freezing, and postcard-perfect.

I tensed my shoulders as the truck approached downtown. I parked in the far corner of the free community parking lot next to the mound of snow the plow had already created, but I didn't open the door. Not yet.

I needed a second.

Of all the people the company could've picked to send here to get one measly signature, it had to be me. I stayed quiet during the presentation. Didn't say a word as the bosses identified the perfect downtown location. Kept it to myself as a million memories arced across my brain the second I saw my hometown flash up on that screen.

It was Darby Crispin who had given me away. With his smug grin, overpriced glasses, and designer suit paid for through his trust fund, he piped up with, "Hey, aren't you from Montana, Creason?"

I'd like to think I wasn't. If I had my way, half my childhood would be erased from my memory and I could pretend I'd lived most of my life in Chicago. But the bosses knew better. Hatfield's eyes lit up and he snapped his fingers as he pointed at me. "Yes! That's right. What town, Creason? Was it near here?"

I should've mumbled Billings or Helena or anything other than Bent Creek, but the company had my information on file. So I confessed to Bent Creek.

And now, here I was. The lucky one who got to "go back home!" as Hatfield put it, and "get that signature!"

I should've put up more of a protest, but I didn't. They expected me to come here and work magic, and if I could, it would mean big things for me. Maybe it wouldn't be so bad, I'd thought.

Until I opened the envelope containing the documents we needed to have signed.

An SUV pulled up next to me, jerking me out of my thoughts. I grabbed the leather folio with the paperwork and jumped out before whoever it was could see me. The last thing I wanted was to get caught up in a conversation with someone I hadn't seen in ten years. Or worse, escape a glare or some other reminder of why I'd left this place.

I needed to focus on what I was doing. Get the impossible signature. Get out.

The snow crunched underfoot as the cold air bit my face. It wasn't exactly warm in Chicago this time of year either, but there was something different about winter in Montana. It was cleaner. Colder. More alive.

I kept my head down as I moved along the sidewalk. It was mid-afternoon, and I was starving. The granola bar I'd scarfed down before boarding the plane in Chicago was a distant memory, and I was too jumpy to even consider lunch when I landed in Billings. I could almost taste the potato soup when I walked past the Snowshoe Cafe. But I didn't dare stop.

I didn't dare make eye contact with anyone who might remember me.

I finally raised my eyes when I reached the corner across from the building I needed to acquire today. And when I did, I sucked in a freezing breath.

This place was the *same*. It was unbelievable. I squinted against the sunlight as I studied the businesses marching up and down Main Street. Half of them had been in business since I was a kid. The lampposts held wreaths as they had every December. The same benches sat here and there, a few inches of snow piled on them.

And yet something was different . . . something I couldn't pinpoint.

Quaint, that was how Hatfield had described Bent Creek. *Ripe for development.* My stomach flipped for the hundredth time since landing in Montana, and I ignored the slight hint of distaste that rose in my mouth at the thought of Hatfield's words.

This wasn't my home anymore, and I needed to remember that. It hadn't been since long before I came to my senses and left. These people didn't want me. They didn't want my family. And I had a job to do—a good, very lucrative one—and if I wanted to keep it, I needed to forget any doubt I had and do what I came here for.

It wasn't until I reached the opposite side of Evergreen Street that I realized what had changed.

I paused again, just outside the building the company wanted to acquire. The lamppost wreaths were a homey shade of green, the strings of lights that would come on at dusk looped here and there, the snow was just as white and crisp as ever.

But there was no one here.

A few people milled up and down Main Street, but it wasn't as I remembered it, especially at this time of year. The ski resorts were teeming with people, and Bent Creek should have been too.

That was why the company wanted this building so badly. It was smack in the middle of town, on the biggest corner lot. They wanted it for cheap because with something new and shiny, the people would come back. They'd spend money. And Durnstorff and Vibert would buy more, build more, and line their pockets.

Ripe for development.

I shoved down the part of me that felt sick about the whole thing. No matter how much I told myself that Bent Creek didn't mean anything to me, that little nostalgic part inside from when I was a kid refused to die. The whole town was glad when my brothers and I trickled out, one by one. That's what I needed to remember.

Now it was like the Harkers were never here. And despite my last name, I was a Harker through and through.

Shoulders steeled, I pressed open the door to Bent Creek Christmas. A cheerful chime jingled, and I walked into Christmas overload. Christmas trees, carols overhead, the faint hint of cinnamon, glinting ornaments, shining lights, smiling Santas, and—I sniffed the air—was that hot chocolate?

The whole place made me want to be five years old again and yet simultaneously throw up that granola bar.

I felt like the hulking linebacker I'd been at seventeen as I ducked to avoid hitting my head on a dangling display of lights and evergreens and red bows. I was pretty sure I wouldn't make it from the door to the cash register without breaking something.

"Hello! Welcome to Bent Creek Christmas!" a low, melodic voice called, and I froze where I was.

It was her.

Of course it was her. What did I expect, to walk into Marybeth Noble's shop and not see her?

"Do you need help finding anything?" she said as she rounded a particularly fat Christmas tree, a length of shiny gold ribbon in her hands.

I was still partially bent down to keep from bumping my head, but I barely noticed how awkwardly I was standing.

She looked the same, just like the girl I'd wanted so badly in high school—and the only one I couldn't, under any circumstances, have. She was tall and lean, like she still ran cross country. Long hair that swung when she walked and was some mysterious shade between red and brown. Hazel eyes framed with dark lashes. And that smile . . .

It flickered for a second when she saw me, like she wasn't sure if the past still mattered.

But it did. The whole plane ride here, I tried to tell myself it wouldn't interfere with the job I came here to do. But I was still Gabe Creason, stepson to Tom Harker.

And she was still Marybeth Noble, daughter of the man who ruined my family.

Chapter Three

Marybeth

"Gabe?" Just saying his name felt strange, and suddenly I was fifteen years old again, with a raging crush on a senior football player.

One whose family my dad had felt owed him for years. He never got payment—he got revenge instead.

Gabe straightened, and his head smashed right into the bough of faux evergreen and lights I had hanging from the ceiling.

"Are you all right?" I asked, and immediately felt stupid. Of course he was okay. It wasn't like the plastic greenery and tiny lights could have hurt him. In fact, it didn't look like much could hurt Gabe Creason at all. He was leaner than he used to be, but he was hardly hurting for muscles, which was saying something considering he was wearing a coat and . . . was that a suit?

"Are you wearing a suit?" I blurted out before I could stop myself.

His eyes—just as blue as I remembered them—narrowed slightly as he swiped uselessly at his hair.

A warmth crawled up my neck into my face, and I wished I could take the observation back. But it *was* surprising. The Gabe I'd known in high school had worked his family's ranch in his off hours. I'd never seen him in anything but jeans, boots, and a hat.

He looked different without the hat.

Gabe gave up swiping at his hair, but bits of plastic greenery still sat among the dark blond strands.

"You still have, um . . ." I pointed at his hair, and when he gave me a confused look, I stood on my tiptoes and pulled the bits of greenery out.

Ignoring the memory of daydreams I'd had as a teenager about running my hands through his hair, I successfully got every piece of fake evergreen out and then awkwardly took a step back.

"Thanks," he said, and the word sounded strange, as if he didn't say it very often. As if he didn't have a wife or a girlfriend to do nice things for him.

I couldn't help it. My gaze wandered down to his left hand. He wasn't wearing gloves, and his ring finger was glaringly bare.

Heat shot up into my face. I turned quickly—hopefully before he noticed—to drop the pieces of greenery into the small trash can behind the counter.

When I turned around, he was right there on the other side of the counter. I guess I hadn't expected him to follow me. I had to swallow the squeak that tried to emerge from my throat at seeing him right there, taking up a lot more space across from me than my mind—or my heart—was ready for.

His gaze traveled around my shop, which gave me a few seconds to pull myself together. When he turned his attention back to me, I gave him a smile again and shoved my hands into the pockets of my jeans just to have something to do with them.

Gabe eyed me coolly, as if he were assessing a fenceline for its sturdiness. I might've had a crush on him ten years ago, but clearly he'd never felt the same way.

And of course he didn't. He probably hated me as much as he hated my father.

The silence stretched out between us until I couldn't stand it any more. "Would you like some peppermint hot chocolate?" I nodded toward the Crock Pot I kept plugged in at the end of the counter.

He looked from me to the hot chocolate station, which I was awfully proud of. I kept it stocked with cute Christmas-themed cups, marshmallows, peppermint sticks, and a can of whipped cream. The customers loved it.

But Gabe frowned. "No, thank you."

"Are you sure?" I reached for a cup. "Everyone loves—"

"I don't like hot chocolate."

"Oh." I set the cup down and started unnecessarily rearranging the display. Who didn't like hot chocolate?

When I finally turned around, I found him eyeing the display of hand-knitted Christmas stockings.

"The knitting circle at the senior center makes those," I said, leaning against the counter to see the display better. "I donate a percentage of each one that sells to the hospital's charity fund."

He frowned at the stockings. Actually frowned!

I was beginning to suspect something about Gabe Creason.

When he turned back toward me, a general expression of distaste written across his obnoxiously handsome face, I tilted my head and confronted him. "You're a Scrooge."

The distaste fell away to confusion, and he lifted his eyebrows. "I'm a what?"

"A Scrooge. You know, from *A Christmas Carol*. Charles Dickens?"

Recognition flickered, and I could have sworn he actually smiled for half a second. "I just don't go in for all of . . . this."

I didn't know what to make of that. "Why would a Scrooge come into a Christmas shop?"

"I'm not a Scrooge." His words sounded irritated, and I felt a little victory in getting under his skin.

Because heaven knew he'd certainly gotten under mine.

"Mmm," I said noncommittally. "You didn't answer the question."

He reached for the fancy leather folio under his arm that I hadn't even noticed before now. But then he paused, turned, and grabbed an ornament off the nearest tree.

"That. I want to buy that." He set the ornament down.

It was a pretty, delicate glass ball that had *Our First Christmas* written in sparkling script. The perfect gift for a cherished significant other.

I swallowed the lump in my throat as I slipped behind the counter. "This is a good choice," I forced myself to say. I kept my eyes on the gift and began wrapping it as I spoke.

He said nothing in return, and I couldn't help myself—I looked up.

And I found him watching me with those eyes that were bluer than the Montana sky in summer.

I swallowed hard, my heart pounding, and tried to finish wrapping up the gift without my hands shaking. When I finished boxing the ornament, I handed it to him the second he reached for it himself. His fingers brushed mine, and it was like touching fire.

I yanked my hand away and busied myself with ringing up the sale.

He paid, and then he was gone without a word, ducking to avoid the evergreen bough this time.

What was that about?

The question rang in my head as I leaned on the counter. I felt as if I'd just finished a run, entirely winded and my heart rate flying.

I pulled out my phone, ready to text Larkin. My fingers hovered over the screen, and then I shoved the phone back into my pocket. For some reason, I wanted to keep this to myself. This whole, strange . . . *thing*.

If anyone had asked me two hours ago if I still had feelings for my high school crush, I would have laughed. It had been a futile thing back then. Even if he'd felt the same way, it never would have happened—not if either one of us had wanted to remain on speaking terms with our families. Dad would have locked me in my room, Mom would have insisted on a heart-to-heart, and my brothers . . . I swallowed at the way things used to be. It wouldn't have ended well at all.

But that had never been an issue, because Gabe was older and he'd never noticed my existence. Then his family situation blew up, he graduated and left, and I'd slowly forgotten about him as my life went on.

And then out of nowhere, ten years later, he walked right into my shop with those arresting eyes and those arms I'd always dreamed of running my hands over. A man who somehow hated Christmas and yet bought a sappy ornament for his girlfriend. While wearing a suit. And barely saying two words to me.

What in the world was he doing back in Bent Creek?

Chapter Four

Gabe

The cold air assaulted my face as I drove out of town with the window down.

And I welcomed it. I needed to think straight, and jacking up the heater wouldn't help with that. My eyes stung from the wind and the sun dancing off the snow. I grabbed blindly in the passenger seat for my sunglasses.

I drove miles out of town before my breathing finally slowed and I felt mostly normal again. And that was when I realized where I'd taken myself.

Quarter Mile Road.

I'd laugh if the memories weren't so dismal. It was like I'd never left, and some part of my brain thought I was going home.

I gripped the steering wheel. It wasn't home anymore.

I could turn around. The road here was narrow, but it wasn't impossible. But some part of me just wanted to get it over with. If I laid eyes on the old ranch now, I wouldn't go back to Chicago and spend years wondering about it.

So I kept driving.

And I kept thinking about the ranch because somehow that seemed better than thinking about Marybeth Noble and her ridiculous Christmas shop.

Even though it had been years since I'd driven this way, I knew the second I passed onto our land.

What *had been* our land, I corrected myself.

It was a huge spread. The land had been in my stepfather's family for generations—until it wasn't anymore. Whoever ended up with it probably couldn't believe their luck. They'd probably made it even more profitable than it had been. It wouldn't have been hard to do with someone entirely focused on the ranch, unlike my distracted Pops.

I drove farther down the road, past the empty snow-covered pastures, until I reached the open gate. Someone had taken down the Harker Ranch sign that used to arch over the driveway. I'd expected that, but no one had hung anything in its place. Instead, the plain wood frame had splintered, and the top piece swayed in the breeze.

I squinted down the drive. The house and the outbuildings weren't set too far back, and there wasn't a car or a truck in sight. The snow covering the driveway was pristine, without a single track.

Curiosity got the best of me. I threw the truck into reverse until I was far enough back to turn into the driveway. Leaving the gate open wasn't smart. Between that and the desiccated state of the arch, a knot developed in my stomach. The tires crunched over the snow as I drove slowly up toward the house.

I reached the barn first. One of the doors hung wide open and a gaping black hole interrupted the white expanse of snow on the roof.

My throat went dry, and I swallowed hard as I pulled my eyes from the ruined barn. It didn't get better as I inched along the driveway. The stable and bunkhouse were in better shape, at least on the outside, but there were no horses in the corral.

And not a soul anywhere to be seen.

I pulled up along the circle in front of the house, and a hundred different emotions hit me at once. Squeezing the steering wheel, I closed my eyes for a second to let them all dissipate before I turned off the truck, opened the door, and stepped outside.

I noticed the silence first. There was no braying of cattle, no men calling across the yard, no nickering of horses, no banging or hammering to fix the endless things that needed fixing on a ranch . . . Nothing at all.

Then I saw the broken window.

The peeling paint.

The gutter that hung from the corner of the roof.

The litter on the porch.

This ranch—my *home*—was abandoned.

I gaped at the house and the outbuildings for a few more minutes, trying to figure out how this happened. After the IRS took the property—since tax fraud was the only meaningful charge the courts could prove beyond a few other minor ones—they sold it. I never got the name of the people who bought it. By then, I'd graduated and gotten out of town as fast I could.

I could text one of my younger brothers that had gone to live with our aunt over in Livingston. Maverick, maybe. He'd be the most likely to know, even though like the rest of us, he'd left the area as soon as he could.

But I hadn't talked to Mav, or any of my stepbrothers, in more years than I could remember.

Maybe it was better that I didn't know, that I didn't lift the lid to the past to see what ghosts came pouring out.

Back in the truck, I threw on the heat and drove down the driveway without looking back. Marybeth's image floated in my mind as I turned left onto Quarter Mile Road. I'd bet everything I had—which, thanks to doing nothing but working since I was eighteen, wasn't insignificant—that Carson Noble's ranch didn't look a thing like the place I just left.

Carson Noble won the war between our families, and with the Harkers out of the way, he'd probably built an empire over the last ten years.

I scowled at the windshield until I remembered it didn't matter anymore. It was ancient history. And now that I was years separated from this place, I could see it for what it was—a stupid feud brought on by two greedy men that landed one of them in prison. And none of it affected me anymore.

As I drove back in toward town, I wondered what Marybeth thought of it all. Did she think it was all as pointless as I did, or did she think her dad was in the right?

She never seemed to care much about it, at least back then. While I wouldn't have wanted to meet any of her brothers while I was alone, Marybeth always had a sweet smile for me. For a while, I'd thought she liked me. It was a crazy thought, of course, and something that never could have happened.

But it had been nice to think about it sometimes back then.

How was she still here? Bent Creek didn't have much to offer beyond ranching and catering to tourists, and given what a ghost town Main Street had been today, that shop she ran couldn't actually be making her money. The bosses seemed to think it'd be easy to convince her to sign. After all, they were offering more than that shop probably turned in profit in five years, and it was still a bargain for them considering how much money they planned to make from the property. It would be a win for both parties.

Yet I couldn't bring myself to ask Marybeth.

I pulled up at the Dowling Bed and Breakfast before I could think very long on the *why* behind my inaction at Marybeth's shop. I grabbed my stuff from the truck and made my way up the steps to the big wraparound porch. The bed and breakfast had been here since I was a kid. Old Mrs. Dowling owned the place, a rambling Victorian style home, and apparently she still did, given the name hadn't changed.

I rang the doorbell as I wished the firm had put me up at a chain hotel closer to the interstate. At least there, no one would have recognized me. I could've relaxed in the comfort of anonymity. Unlike here . . .

Mrs. Dowling answered the door with a beaming smile. "Come in, come in!" She held the door open wide.

I slipped inside to a welcoming warmth and the faint scent of apples. A wreath adorned the little desk near the door, Christmas music played quietly over an unseen sound system, pine boughs and ribbons danced up the grand staircase, and a giant tree stood in the parlor room just off to the right.

It was like Marybeth's shop had come in here and exploded.

"Here, let me take that, Tom." Mrs. Dowling reached for my bag.

And I was stunned enough to hand it to her. *Tom*. I didn't look a thing like my stepfather. I didn't even share his last name. And yet—

"I was so sorry to hear about Katrina's passing. You must be heartbroken. I know how it feels." She reached out and patted my arm with a weathered hand and offered me a kind, sad smile.

My heart clenched and I bit down on the inside of my cheek. Katrina was my mother. She'd died years ago, when I was eight. A whopping three years after marrying Tom Harker.

I didn't know what to say. Was I supposed to correct her? Let it go?

"Gran?" Suzanne Dowling, Mrs. Dowling's granddaughter appeared in the doorway to the parlor with a baby on her hip.

"Hmm?" Mrs. Dowling was still looking at me with sympathy.

"Gran, why don't you let me take care of our new guest? That way you can get back to the soup." Suzanne shifted the baby and smiled at her grandmother.

"The soup, yes. I'll do that." Mrs. Dowling looked at me again, shook her head, and disappeared back into the house.

"Gabe." Suzanne said my name in a pleasant voice as she approached the desk. "I'm so sorry about that. Gran gets . . . confused sometimes. I hope she didn't upset you."

I shook my head, even though it had been disconcerting to be reminded of Mom so suddenly. It was bound to come at some point while I was here, so why not from a sweet old woman with memory troubles? It could've been worse.

Suzanne dug out an old-fashioned key and handed it to me. "You're in Room 5, top of the stairs." She paused and the baby cooed. "It's good to see you again, Gabe. You look different." Her eyes swept me up and down, and I could almost hear Marybeth's question in her thoughts—*Why are you wearing a suit?*

"Thanks." I turned the key over in my hand. "Good to see you, too. What's the baby's name?" I asked the question more to distract her from me and why I was there more than anything else.

She smiled at the baby. "This is Annie." And when Suzanne looked back at me, I realized how much older she looked. Maybe not *older*, really, but more worn. Tired. As if she'd been through life in a serious way since her days as a varsity cheerleader.

"Thanks," I said, holding up the key.

"We serve breakfast from seven to nine," she called after me. "I'm looking forward to catching up with you."

I held up a hand to acknowledge her. And then I shut myself in Room 5, with all my thoughts about the ranch and Marybeth Noble and no place to hide from them.

Chapter Five

Marybeth

I frowned at myself in the mirror. I looked exhausted no matter how much concealer I used. I forced a smile at myself and wondered what Gabe had seen yesterday—stressed Marybeth or happy Marybeth?

I *was* happy, mostly. When I didn't worry about the shop or question every decision I'd ever made.

If I focused on what mattered—keeping the shop afloat, helping Luke with the ranch when he needed me, helping Larkin with Diego—things would work out. I knew they would.

They had to.

In the kitchen, Luke was already done with a bowl of cereal and half the pot of coffee. I poured myself a cup, added a generous helping of cream and fake sugar, and sat down across from my older brother. I studied him for a moment. He looked worlds better than he had two years ago, when he'd lost his wife.

"Are the roofers coming today?" I asked, cradling the warm mug in my hands.

Luke shrugged and looked up from his phone. "They're supposed to. Almost hope they don't. I've got a list a mile long that needs getting done."

"If it's not busy, I'll close up early and come home to help." There was a time when all I wanted was for Luke to get out of bed and have breakfast. The fact that he was now worried about balancing a to-do list was a victory I'd had a hard time hoping for back then.

Luke nodded absentmindedly, another sign that he was effectively running this place on his own again. His eyes went back to his phone, and I thought I ought to call Mom and Dad. They'd be happy to hear something like this, as mundane as it was. I stood and rummaged through the fridge until I found a cup of yogurt. When I turned around, Luke was looking at me.

"Gabe Creason's back in town," he said. "Did you see him yesterday?"

I froze, yogurt in hand and my mind spinning. Did someone tell him Gabe came into my store? The whole . . . *thing* . . . between our families was so long ago, and the Harkers clearly got the losing end. Tom Harker was in prison, and Mom and Dad had moved to Florida. What did it matter if Gabe showed up in Bent Creek and went to my shop?

I opted for the truth. "Yes," I said, my voice perfectly even as I set my yogurt on the table and went for a spoon. "He came into the store and bought an ornament for his girlfriend."

"Why is he here?"

When I turned around, Luke was watching me like I knew the answer to his question.

"I don't know. He didn't exactly confide in me." I sounded dismissive, but inside I was a mess. My heart was beating overtime and I wasn't sure I'd ever catch my breath again. It was like Luke had caught me and Gabe together, which was not only impossible, but a completely nonexistent thing.

"It doesn't make sense. There's nothing here for them, not anymore. What's left of that ranch is a magnet for teenagers and vandals. Can't believe I couldn't get my hands on it." Luke glanced at his phone again and picked it up to answer a text.

I took that moment to sit down and occupy myself with opening my yogurt. Why *was* Gabe here? It was a question I'd asked myself a hundred times since yesterday. "Maybe he just came to visit."

Luke made a face as he typed. He knew as well as I did that the Harkers didn't have a whole lot of friends in town, not anymore. Not after everyone found out what Mr. Harker had been up to.

"I don't like that he came to your shop," Luke said as he sat his phone down.

"Seriously?" I looked up at my brother. "It wasn't anything. All he wanted was an ornament." Okay, maybe it had felt like more than that, but I wasn't about to admit that to Luke. Especially since I didn't know *what* exactly it was at all.

Luke stood. "I've got to meet the men before the roofers get here. If Creason shows up at your shop again, call me." He paused as I lifted my eyebrows. "I'm dead serious, Marybeth. He could be dangerous."

Dangerous. I nodded at my brother, which must have satisfied him enough since he went to the back door.

The second he was gone, I sat back in my chair, letting my shoulders slump. I'd be naive if I didn't grudgingly admit that Luke was at least a little right. Gabe and his brothers had always flirted with the edge of danger. It was half sexy and half terrifying. And it all made sense when the whole town found out the rumors about their family were more than rumors. When my dad put his in prison.

Gabe Creason could be here to relive old memories—or he could be here for revenge. And I had to remember that.

I finished my yogurt and grabbed my bag and my purse. I wanted to get into town early to see Larkin before I opened the store.

My trusty old Honda SUV chugged to life. Every day I didn't have to buy a new car was a good day. I backed out of the garage—the best addition to this house that Luke had built when he took over the ranch from Dad—and paused for a moment before heading down the driveway.

Maybe Gabe was here because of the old Harker ranch property. I knew exactly how much work it took to keep this place going, and I couldn't help feeling bad that Gabe's old home was in such disrepair. Luke had even made an attempt to buy it this past summer, but whoever owned it wouldn't sell. Maybe Gabe was here to change that.

Luke wouldn't be happy about that, but it brought a smile to my face. I'd always thought the way Dad pitted our family against theirs was a waste of energy, and when it had blown up like it did, I felt weirdly responsible. Not for Mr. Harker being accused of tax fraud or a million other things, but for the way it affected his sons.

It didn't seem right, the way they'd lost everything.

I found Larkin pouring a latte for Kyle Clemmons, who had a real estate office in town and who was the only one who'd bested Larkin in the elementary school spelling bee. Diego came running around the counter. I held out my arms and gave him a big squeeze.

"Maybet! I help Mama." He beamed at me, and I couldn't help smiling back even as my stomach sunk. Larkin's boss wasn't exactly the most understanding about her situation, and if he walked in here while Diego was running around, she might not have a job any longer.

I waved at Kyle as Diego ran back around the counter. Larkin held out a hand for my mug. Buying the Mountain Roasters mug was well worth the overpriced cost when it got me free refills.

"Did your mom get called in to work again?" I asked her as Diego handed me two yellow packets of my favorite sweetener.

"Yeah." Larkin sounded completely exhausted. "I've got to find someone else, but I barely make enough to cover my part of our bills. I don't know how I'd pay them."

My heart ached for my friend. "What time do you get off? It should be quiet in the shop this morning. I could take him for a while." I hated admitting that business wasn't what I wanted it to be, but at least that meant I could help Larkin.

Relief washed over her face. "Noon. Could you? I hate asking you, Marybeth. I know it's not easy to keep an eye on him when you've got other things to do."

I waved a hand. Diego could be a handful, but his presence kept me from worrying too much about the future. "It's fine."

She handed me my coffee and sent Diego to get his coat. With Diego buttoned up with a too-big hat on and his little hands stuffed into mittens, we headed down the street. And I realized I never got to tell her about Gabe.

Gabe—who was now standing outside my shop like he couldn't wait to get inside and buy another ornament.

Chapter Six

Gabe

The second I saw her again, I wanted to bolt.

No one should look that adorable bundled up in a coat with clunky snow boots and a hat with a pom pom. And yet somehow, Marybeth Noble did as she came down the sidewalk with a little boy holding her hand.

I didn't know she had a child.

She stopped in front of me, her cheeks red with the cold and her breath forming little clouds, while those green-brown eyes searched my face.

"Good morning, Gabe," she said in a voice laced with curiosity.

"Gabe!" The little boy at her side repeated my name. He was as cute as she was. Kids usually made me want to run away, with their sticky fingers and nonsensical stories, but there was something about this kid, with his big brown eyes and innocent smile, that reminded me of myself.

And if that wasn't weird enough, I had to swallow the disappointment that rose inside me at knowing Marybeth was probably married. I didn't know who the guy was, but I somehow hated and admired him at the same time.

"Good morning," I said stiffly.

She fished a key from her purse and stepped forward to unlock the door. "Did you come to buy another ornament for your girlfriend?"

My girlfriend? My mind went blank. What was she talking about?

Marybeth glanced up at me as she opened the door. "You know, the ornament you bought yesterday? 'Our First Christmas?'"

She led the little boy through the door as the memory came crashing back. I hadn't even looked at the ornament before plucking it off the tree in a moment of desperation. If I hadn't chickened out and just gotten her signature, I wouldn't have bought that gaudy tree decoration.

"It wasn't—" I paused as I ducked under that giant pine bough, trying to figure out how to save face. "It was a gift. For a friend. And, uh . . . his girlfriend."

"Oh!" She gave me an unreadable look as she set her stuff on the counter, and for a moment, I hoped she was happy to learn I hadn't bought that ornament for any woman in my life.

I was suddenly too hot, standing here in a coat. I unzipped the heavy parka while she wrestled the little boy out of his coat.

"Color?" he asked as she plucked the hat from his head.

"Of course." She plopped a kiss onto his chubby cheek, went behind the counter, and emerged with some paper and crayons. She settled him into a corner with such attention and tenderness that it reminded me of my own mother.

I swallowed the lump in my throat, and when she stood and turned to look back at me, I blurted out, "You're a good mom."

She blinked at me and then laughed. "Thank you, I guess, but Diego isn't mine. I'm not . . . I don't have . . . I mean . . ." Her face colored. "He's Larkin's son. You remember Larkin Reyes?"

I nodded mutely. I remembered Larkin—she'd gone out with my brother Nick for a solid year or so in high school. But mostly I was relieved to know that Marybeth didn't have some guy waiting for her at home. Or at least that's what I wanted to believe she meant before she went on to tell me about Larkin.

"Larkin had this boyfriend," Marybeth said as she grabbed her things from the counter. "He turned out to be a nightmare. I still don't know what she saw in him. Anyway, he was gone faster than a summer storm when he found out she was pregnant, and well . . ." Marybeth glanced at Diego.

I nodded again and wondered what Nick would think about that. I wasn't sure what to say, but mostly I was taken with the way that Marybeth cared for Diego like he was her own. How no one in this town had managed to claim her yet was something I'd never understand. And yet it made me happier than it should have.

"You lost the suit." Her voice yanked me from thoughts I had no business thinking.

"Yeah." I self-consciously shoved my hands into the pockets of my jeans.

Her eyes traveled the length of me and I felt the strangest urge to ask if she approved.

"I like it better," she said with a smile. "It's more . . . you."

Well, that was curious. "How would you know that?"

Her cheeks went pink and she ducked her head, pretending to study something on the papers stacked next to her cash register. It made me want to take the two steps left between me and that counter, lean over it and—

"I don't know. Just that your family are ranchers, and . . . yeah." She didn't look up. Her red-brown hair hid her face, but I imagined she was still blushing.

"Were," I corrected her. "We *were* ranchers."

She looked up then. Her lips pinched together, as if she was thinking about what to say next. "I know." Her voice was soft. "I . . . I'm sorry."

It should have made me angry. Pops would've wanted me to be furious. But I couldn't summon it. Not after all this time, for something I had a hard time feeling even back then. And not at Marybeth.

Instead, I took those last two steps until I was at that counter. It was sprinkled in bits of glitter, probably shed from dozens and dozens of overpriced, silly tree ornaments and useless ribbon. "Don't be."

Her brow furrowed. "Don't be what?"

"Sorry. It's not your fault."

Her fingers curled against the edge of the counter, and the crazy part of me wanted to reach over and grab hold of her hands. Tell her I didn't care about the history between our families. And that I'd meant what I said. None of it was her fault.

It wasn't mine either.

She held my gaze for a moment. "Have you been out there?"

I knew exactly what she meant, and the thought of it made my stomach turn. I nodded quickly, not trusting my voice.

"Luke tried to buy it a couple of years ago. He thought it would be a good expansion for us. But they wouldn't sell."

"Your *brother* tried to buy my family's land?" History was in the past, but it didn't stop the lick of fire that lit up inside me at that piece of information.

Marybeth took a tiny step back. "He wasn't the first one. They won't sell to anyone. I don't know why."

Whoever owned the place preferred to let it fall apart. The anger burned more than I would have liked it to. More than it should have.

Because it didn't matter what Pops did or didn't do. That property was supposed to belong to me and my brothers. And now it was a wreck, lying useless and empty.

Marybeth watched me, sorrow and curiosity in her eyes. It was a look I remembered well. One I'd gotten over and over again between my stepdad's arrest and the day I finally left Bent Creek.

I came here to do a job, not lose myself in a pretty girl I had no business being interested in anyway. It was a job I was good at. And it was time I closed this deal and got back to it.

I yanked the folio from under my arm and plunked it down on the counter. Marybeth jumped slightly, and guilt tried to creep its way into my mind.

No. I had nothing to feel guilty about.

I flipped open the cover, pulled the pen from its sheath, and turned it so Marybeth could read the pages. "This is why I'm here." I laid the pen on the first page of the contract for sale.

She skimmed the words, and when she looked up at me, I barely recognized her.

Fury colored her expression, turning down those pink lips and shading her eyes.

"You work for them? For . . ." She glanced down at the first page. "Durnstorff and Vibert?" Her voice had gone cold, but there was no mistaking the tremor that sat beneath the words.

She hated me right now.

I looked down at the papers and pointed to them. "We've upped the offer. It's more than you'd get selling this place to someone in town."

"Why? What does some development firm in Chicago want with this old building in Bent Creek?"

I forced myself to meet her gaze. The job. I had to think about the job. "We see potential here, especially with the new developments in the resort towns. Bent Creek can't compete with that, not unless it modernizes."

"Modernizes?" She lifted a single eyebrow, mocking me in just one single word.

"Yes."

"So you want to rip down this historic building and replace it with what? A Cheesecake Factory? A Sephora? A Bass Pro Shop?" She laughed, a hollow sound that meant anything but amusement.

"No," I said, hating that she'd put me on the defensive. "Look, I'll be honest. I don't know what they want to put here. But it's something that will draw tourists and help the town."

"Because my shop doesn't," she said flatly.

"That's not what I said."

"That's what I heard." She crossed her arms.

She was being stubborn, and irritation finally consumed my guilt. I threw my arms open. "How many people do you have in here? Besides me, you, and the kid in the corner? How much have you sold this month? Enough to cover your expenses? Or are you in this business to lose money?"

Marybeth glared at me. I wondered if she kept a pistol under her counter, because if she did, I half-expected her to pull it out now and aim it at me.

She held my gaze for a moment. Then, in one swift movement, she slammed the folio shut and shoved it at my chest. The pen fell to the counter, and I grabbed the papers before they fluttered out all over the floor.

"I will *never* sign that. I wouldn't sell to your firm if I was starving. Get out of my shop." She pointed to the door.

The little boy watched us from his corner, his eyes perfectly round. I took my time arranging the papers inside the folio, picked up the pen, and then met her eyes.

I wanted to say something. To convince her this was the right thing for her to do.

But I said nothing at all.

Instead, I turned, tucked the papers back under my arm, and headed for the door. My hand on the knob, I turned back. She stood there, arms crossed again, watching me.

"Just so you know, I wear a suit every day back in Chicago." And before she could say anything else, I pressed the door open and stepped outside into the freezing cold.

The wind bit at my face and the cold wrapped itself around me where my coat was still open. But I barely felt it. Because all I could think of was how stupid I must have sounded—and how much I hated my job right now.

Chapter Seven

Marybeth

"M aybet okay?"

I lifted my face out of my hands to see Diego's adorable face looking up at me in toddler concern. I forced yet another smile. "I'm fine, sweetie. That man just made me angry for a little bit, but I'm okay now."

Satisfied, he brought me the papers he'd colored, and I oohed and aahed over his scribbles. Then he followed me around while I got the shop ready to open, distracting me from thoughts of Gabe.

I got the peppermint hot chocolate made and set Diego up with a tiny little tree in the corner and a box full of homemade ornaments from my childhood. He was having a blast hanging them all on one side of the tree when Carol Foley, who used to babysit me and my brothers when we were little, came in.

Seeing her lifted my spirits. She came in about once a month for the exact same thing—seasonal cookie decorations. Her mission in life was to distribute home-baked cookies to everyone she thought could use a little cheering up. Even though I ran a Christmas shop, I kept a small stock of seasonally appropriate cookie cutters, sprinkles, and more, mostly for Mrs. Foley and the other bakers in town.

I greeted her with a smile. "Just wait until you see these new cookie cutters I got." I wound my way through the shop, around trees and displays, until I reached the baking shelves. I searched through the newly stocked display of Christmas-related cookie items until I found what I was looking for. "Voila!" I held out the cutest set of "Jingle Bells" themed cookie cutters.

Mrs. Foley examined them, and a smile lit up her face. "I think I like the horse the best. These are great, Marybeth. I just need to collect a few other things."

I stepped away to let her choose, peeked at Diego who was trying to top the tiny tree with his snow boot, and tried to busy myself with the stack of papers on the counter. Some of it was junk, some of it was important—and now it all reminded me of the contract Gabe tried to convince me to sign.

How had a quiet, handsome cowboy like Gabe Creason turned into a slimy developer?

When he left town, I'd felt a strange sort of sadness. I wasn't surprised when Gabe and Nick, his oldest stepbrother, left right after they'd graduated. But it had still hurt. I'd been fifteen, plenty old enough to know I never stood a chance with him, but still young enough to harbor a serious crush. I'd imagined him running off to Wyoming or Texas, joining up to work another ranch somewhere. Maybe training horses, or even coaching football.

But never in my wildest dreams had I pictured him in Chicago. Wearing a suit. Working to obliterate the character of little towns like Bent Creek.

I'd *never* sell Bent Creek Christmas to someone like that. I didn't care if I didn't have a cent to my name. I'd rather go bankrupt than let some greedy city development company rip this place down and tear out part of the heart of this town. And if Gabe thought he could throw money in my face and flash those eyes at me and make me go weak in the knees like I was fifteen again, he—

"Marybeth?" Mrs. Foley was standing at the counter while I was lost in thought.

I shoved Gabe from my mind and looked down at Mrs. Foley's purchases. "Did you find what you needed?"

"I did. I love these little red and gold chocolates." She tilted her head. "You seemed lost in thought."

"I was, a little," I admitted as I entered her items into the register. My heart thumped. What would this town think if they knew how much I'd wished Gabe had shown up at my door this morning because he wanted to see *me*?

It was such an embarrassing thought after learning why he was really here.

"Is it Luke?" she asked gently.

I shook my head. "No, he's doing really well."

"I'm glad to hear that." She paused. "Is it a person, or something else? What's bothering you, I mean."

"A little bit of both," I said as I reached for a paper bag.

"Ah," she said as if she understood completely. "Well, Christmas will be here soon, and it can warm even the coldest of hearts."

A shiver ran through me as I thought of Gabe's distaste for my store and everything in it.

"I'm not so sure about that, but I wish it was true." I handed her the bag.

"Have faith, Marybeth." She patted my arm. "I'll be sure to bring you a cookie when they're baked. And one for the little guy, too. You're doing a good thing, helping his mama like you do."

I thanked her and watched her leave with a smile. Mrs. Foley's visit was just what I needed, even though I didn't necessarily think she was right.

Gabe was long past having a warm heart.

Chapter Eight

Gabe

The text came in while I was standing in the abandoned driveway at the ranch.

Status on Montana project?

Colin Hatfield. Just seeing his name attached to the text made me feel like I was on edge.

Working on it. That's all I could stomach typing. He didn't need to know about Marybeth, or the history between our families, or the fact that I was standing here on what used to be Harker land and wishing I'd never left.

I'd been so sure it was the right thing back then. No one wanted us here. We were a disgrace, thanks to Pops. I heard the whispers everywhere I went, and the tax fraud was the least of the town's worries.

It was the drugs that made them look askance at us. It was never proven and the charges were dropped in favor of the sure thing and some minor stuff just to add time to the sentence, but none of that mattered. Because it was all true.

Pops never said as much, but I knew. I think we all knew. We just didn't dare admit it to ourselves or each other. Even Nick and Jackson, who knew more than the rest of us.

But if I'd stayed, maybe this never would have happened to the ranch. Maybe Nick and I could have scraped together some money and bought it somehow.

My mind wandered back to Marybeth. She'd mentioned people had tried to buy it, including her own brother. But whoever owned it wouldn't sell.

Why was that? They clearly didn't care about the place.

My phone buzzed again with another question from Hatfield. I sent back a short response before climbing back in the truck to warm up. A squirrel jumped from the big pine out front as I started the truck. The same tree Mom decorated every year for Christmas before the cancer got her for good.

The memory floated through my head—large shining ornaments, lights of every color, my brother Colt crying when Mom told him we couldn't put a star on the top—and I smiled at it.

It hadn't all been bad. And this place deserved a lot more than it was getting right now.

I put the truck in reverse and turned around, trying to force my mind from the past to the present. I needed to try again with Marybeth. Hatfield wasn't going to wait long, and if I cared about my job, I needed to act faster.

I needed to get this done and haul myself back to Chicago.

I frowned at that thought. There was nothing waiting there for me but an empty apartment and an office I wasn't exactly enthusiastic about walking into again.

The strangest part was, I didn't really know why. It wasn't like there was anything for me here either, or anywhere else.

Marybeth's image floated through my mind again as I dodged a small snowbank. She was so angry at me, and yet I felt this urge to see her again. She probably would pull that pistol I suspected she had if I showed up again.

For some reason, that thought made me smile.

I really was losing my mind.

I ran a hand over my face and tried to think. There was no way that shop was doing well. She had to need the money, unless she was earning something from the ranch. But it sounded like the ranch was Luke's, the oldest. The one who'd tried to buy my land.

Marybeth needed to sell. It made good business sense. I just had to convince her.

Easy, right?

I laughed at myself as I pulled into town.

After I parked the truck, I detoured to the coffee shop. If I was going to show up again, maybe I could smooth it over with coffee.

Larkin Reyes stood behind the counter, and I almost turned around and left, but she saw me first.

"Gabe Creason," she said with an air of curiosity mixed with amusement. "I'd heard you were back in town."

I swallowed, wondering who exactly she'd heard that from.

"Marybeth mentioned it," she said, as if she'd read my mind.

"Great," I muttered under my breath.

That drew an even more curious look, but to her credit, she merely reached for a cup and asked if I wanted coffee.

"Two, please." I fished my wallet from my pocket and pressed my card to the reader.

"Hmm," she said as she poured the second cup.

I didn't dare ask what that meant. I wasn't sure I wanted to know.

Larkin added a generous amount of creamer and two packets of Splenda to one cup and then looked up at me. "What do you take in yours?"

"Nothing. Just black," I said, shoving my wallet back in my pocket and still wondering why she'd doctored the second cup to an overly sweet blend.

"Should've guessed." She passed me both cups and winked at me. "Good luck, and hey, a word of advice? Be a little nicer this time. Diego calls you the Mean Man now."

I caught my jaw before it dropped and hightailed it out of there. The Mean Man? And how did she know I was taking this coffee to Marybeth?

This town, I *swear*. At least she didn't ask me about Nick. Or hold the way he left her here against me.

I was steps away from Marybeth's store when an older woman emerged carrying a tote bag.

"Gabriel Creason," she said with a crinkled smile. "It's good to see you again. Here. I believe you need these."

And before I could react, she shoved a plastic bag filled with cookies between two of my fingers. It dangled there as I tried to hang on to both the bag and the coffee. *Mrs. Foley*, I remembered as she walked away.

Why in the world did the old woman who used to work at the bank just give me cookies?

Shaking my head, I pushed open the door to the shop with my shoulder. This town could be sickeningly sweet sometimes. Maybe that was why my family never really fit in here.

That was an excuse for Dad's actions, and I knew it, but it felt good to think it for a minute. It was better than thinking about the fact that not a single person acted the way I'd expected since I got here.

"I thought I told you to get out of my store."

Marybeth stood right there by the door, her hands on her hips and looking for all the world like she'd push me right back out if she thought she could.

The text from Hatfield, the abandoned ranch, this town . . . everything on my mind seemed to disappear with her gaze on me.

And all I wanted to do was throw the coffee and cookies aside, grab hold of her, and kiss her until she understood I was trying to help her.

Chapter Nine

Marybeth

"Cookies? Coffee?" Gabe held up one of his hands, filled with a cup from Mountain Roasters and a bag with Christmas cookies from Mrs. Foley.

And even though I knew what he was here for, I couldn't keep the grin from my lips. "Those are your cookies. Mrs. Foley only gives them to people who need cheering up."

He glanced down at the bag. "I look like I need cheering up?"

"Apparently I did too." I tossed my chin toward the counter, where a bag of sugar cookies decked out in red and gold candy shell chocolates waited for me.

The ghost of a smile found Gabe's face as he took in the cookies. "Coffee, then? Larkin murdered it for you."

I shouldn't take coffee from the man trying to buy up my store just to destroy it, but I could use the caffeine. It had been another impossibly slow day, and the worry was starting to build to a constant hum in the back of my head.

"Let me guess," I said, taking the coffee from him. "Yours is black."

"Yes . . .?" He spoke the word like he couldn't figure out how I knew.

"It matches your personality." I turned and made my way back to the counter to pry the lid off my cup so the coffee could cool some more.

"Is that how Larkin knew? What does that mean?" He cast the questions at my back, and I bit my lip. This was the most I'd ever heard Gabe Creason speak in my life.

And the words were all for me.

Stop it, I warned myself, and yet I couldn't stop grinning. I turned around and leaned against the counter just in time to see Gabe duck under the evergreen bough again. I tried not to think of plucking the bits of plastic greenery from his hair, tried not to envision myself running my hands through it, tried especially hard not to imagine his hands reaching around my back to pull me close—

"I'm not the villain you think I am," he said, stopping next to the tree I'd decorated in a patriotic Christmas theme.

I blinked at him, my brain attempting to catch up to his words as my heart still beat hard enough I was certain he could hear it. Villain . . . the coffee . . . his personality . . . Was he a villain?

"Aren't you?" I said carefully. "You want me to sell my shop to you so you can tear it down and build some soulless development. That's basically a villain in a Hallmark movie."

He scrunched up his forehead like he had no idea what I was talking about. "I'm not the firm I work for."

"Sure. And I hate Christmas."

He clenched his jaw. "It's a job, Marybeth, that's all."

Goosebumps traced their way up my arms when he said my name. I crossed them, thankful I'd worn a sweater. "Could have fooled me."

He narrowed his eyes and took a step forward. "Or is it more than just my job?"

I knew what he was getting at. Luke's warning ran through the back of my mind. *He could be dangerous.* I saw how Luke thought that, based on Gabe's family and his sheer size and the way my brothers and his were always getting into it.

But when I looked into his eyes, I didn't see danger. I saw something else entirely. Sadness. Regret. Ambition. Confusion. And something that burned hotter than I dared think about.

I held his gaze, dropping my arms to my sides. "It's not."

"Are you sure?"

He was much too close now, and if I didn't put some space between us, I wouldn't be able to form a rational thought. "Yes. And I know how you can prove it to me."

His eyebrows lifted. "Prove what?"

"That you aren't a villain." I slid down the counter and away from him, drawing in great gulps of air as I moved quickly toward the rear of the store. I felt him following behind me, and I chewed my lip, glad I'd made him too curious to stay put. "I'll be right back," I said before I slipped into the storeroom in the back.

When I emerged, arms filled with a box of ornaments, multiple spools of ribbon, and extra bulbs for mini lights, his eyes went as round as if I'd brought out a tiger instead.

"What's that?" he asked.

I didn't answer. Instead, I pointed toward the storeroom door after I'd set the box down. "Can you bring out the tree near the back of the room? And the ladder too?"

He eyed me warily for a moment before slipping into the store-room. He emerged a moment later, awkwardly carrying the seven foot tall tree I hadn't set out yet.

"Over there." I pointed toward the back corner of the shop.

"Don't you think you have enough trees in this place?" He grunted as he set the tree down.

"It's a Christmas shop. There can never be enough trees." I flashed him an angelic smile.

What I got in return was a scowl worthy of any good villain. Still, he went to get the ladder without me needing to remind him. He set it down by the tree before he wrestled his coat off.

No suit today either, I noticed. Instead, he wore a flannel shirt over a pair of worn jeans and a pair of boots that looked like they'd be right at home on a ranch.

"Here." I handed him a spool of white ribbon with silvery snowflakes. "This tree is snow-themed."

"What am I supposed to do with this?" He ran a hand through his hair as he held the ribbon at arm's length.

"Wind it around the tree."

"Are you serious?"

"You do that, and I'll plug in the lights." The tree was prelit, so all I had to do was grab the cord and crawl under the tree to plug it in.

When I crawled back out, I found Gabe glaring at the tree. I shifted my gaze to see his work—and covered my mouth to stifle a laugh.

"It looks like—" I had to stop and cover my mouth again. "Like you TP'ed the tree with ribbon."

He turned his scowl toward me, his eyes that same deep blue that had mesmerized me as a teenager. "And you're calling *me* the villain."

"I'm sorry!" I couldn't help it now, and I bent over laughing. When I finally straightened up, I saw him smiling.

"Here," he said, tossing me the ribbon. "You work your magic and I'll hold the ladder."

"Hold the ladder? I'm pretty sure I can—"

"Please just shut up and let me prove I can be a gentleman." He grabbed hold of the ladder.

I shook my head and climbed up. Pulling away the ribbon he'd hung, I wound it back around the spool.

"Does your house look like this too?" he asked.

I glanced down at him, and he threw out a hand to gesture at my shop. "Full of trees and stuff," he said.

I wanted to laugh, but it died in my throat. "No, not really. One tree is about all Luke can stand, and even that takes twisting his arm."

Gabe looked like he wanted to know more, but he wisely kept his questions to himself. As curious as I was about him, I wasn't sure I wanted to tell him about my family's issues or why I lived on the ranch instead of at my own place.

He'd managed to hook one piece of the ribbon around a branch, and I tugged, trying to get it to let go.

"Careful," Gabe said as I pulled again.

"I'm fine. I just need to—" I yanked again, and it came loose. But I'd pulled too hard, and before I could grab hold of the ladder, I went toppling backward.

Right into Gabe's arms.

Chapter Ten

Gabe

It was a split second decision to step around the ladder. Marybeth landed in my outstretched arms.

She drew in a gasp as I stumbled just slightly. I shifted her weight so that one of my arms was under her back and the other one slipped beneath her knees.

"Are you all right?" My voice came out strangled as she pressed a hand against my chest.

She nodded, her eyes wide. I should have put her down. She was okay. Safe. Unhurt. And yet . . . I didn't want to. It felt natural, like she belonged there, protected in my arms.

Her breath warmed my face, and all I could think was that if I leaned down just a few more inches, my lips would meet hers. What would she do if I kissed her? Would she push me away, call me a villain, and kick me out?

Or would she pull me closer and return the kiss?

"Gabe?" Her voice came out shaky and her hand was warm against my shirt.

I groaned inwardly. I had to set her down. Now. Or I didn't know what would happen next. And I didn't trust myself to make that kind of judgment right now.

I lowered my right arm until her feet touched the ground. She stepped away and pulled at her sweater, smoothed her hands over her jeans. "Thank you," she said quietly.

I cleared my throat. I needed to get out here. The carols playing overhead, the trees, the vanilla scent I swore I could smell on Marybeth . . . It was too much.

Everything here was too much.

"I'll see you later." I grabbed my coat and left as fast as I could.

Outside, the frozen air stung my nostrils as I strode quickly down the sidewalk. I was halfway through the next block before I yanked my coat on. I passed more people than I had since I'd arrived back in town as I tried not to think about Marybeth. They each stared at me, more curious than angry, a couple said hello, but I didn't stop until I reached the truck.

But I didn't feel like driving. I left it in the parking lot and walked the blocks back to the bed and breakfast, relishing the cold air hitting my face and burning my lungs. It felt good. It made me feel *alive*. And it clarified my thoughts about Marybeth.

I'd wanted to kiss her. *Badly*. And I couldn't. Not because of our families. None of mine was left here to care, and if Luke Noble or any of her other brothers wanted to have words with me after all this time, so be it.

I couldn't kiss her because I wanted her to sign that contract.

Didn't I?

I climbed the steps to the B&B's porch, my breath coming fast from the pace I'd set walking back. My phone buzzed before I could reach for the door.

With an odd hope it was Marybeth—did she even have my number?—I pulled it out. Only to find a text from Hatfield.

Spoke with Durnstorff. He's concerned. It's been three days. You should be on a flight home with that signature.

A sour taste rose in my mouth. I shoved the phone back into my pocket, wiped the snow from my boots on the scrubber by the door, and went inside without answering Hatfield.

"Hello, Gabriel!" Mrs. Dowling's voice floated in from the parlor where she sat drinking tea with Suzanne.

She knew who I was today. She watched me with clear eyes as I hung up my coat and crossed into the parlor.

"Good morning, Mrs. Dowling." I stood by the door until Suzanne gestured to a nearby chair. I sat. It felt good to be wanted. Suzanne and her grandmother didn't seem to care about what my family had done.

"You left before breakfast." Mrs. Dowling made it sound as if skipping her breakfast was the worst possible thing I could have done.

"I'm sorry," I replied. "I had work I needed to do."

"Would you like some tea?" Suzanne asked.

"No, thank you." I didn't think I'd ever had tea in my life. And I wasn't about to accept a cup now and have to choke it down if I didn't like it.

"What sort of work do you do, Gabriel?" Mrs. Dowling asked, picking up her cup of tea.

The way she called me by my entire first name reminded me of Mom. I braced for the wave of sadness, but it didn't come. Instead I felt . . . reassured. Or maybe comforted, like someone was still looking out for me.

It was an odd thought, and I dug my fingers into the edges of the chair's arms as I tried to figure out how to answer Mrs. Dowling's question without giving away exactly what I was trying to do here in Bent Creek.

Because apparently Marybeth hadn't made it known.

"He works for a company in Chicago, Gran," Suzanne said. "Real estate?"

When I nodded, because that was close enough, she gave me a sheepish look.

"Sorry, I was curious and Googled it when they made the reservation for you."

"Where's Annie?" I asked as my phone buzzed again in my pocket. I didn't pull it out.

"Napping." Suzanne took a sip of tea, and not for the first time, I wondered which of the many boyfriends she'd had in high school might be Annie's father. Bent Creek wasn't exactly a town that saw a lot of permanent newcomers.

Another couple of guests strode by at that moment and Mrs. Dowling waved as they left out the front door.

"How is the B&B doing?" I asked cautiously. Given the lack of traffic at Marybeth's shop and on Main Street, I couldn't imagine it was any different here.

Suzanne shrugged. "We're hanging on."

I took that to mean that business wasn't exactly booming. The firm's development would help that. Desirable new businesses would draw in the tourists, that was a certainty.

But at what cost?

They'd want to stay at an equally trendy hotel. Or a mountain resort style place with a gourmet chef and state of the art exercise equipment, not a quaint old B&B,

I swallowed and looked down at my hands. This development wouldn't just take a corner of downtown—it would change the *entire* town.

Was it for the best?

I honestly didn't know, but I had a hard time looking Suzanne or Mrs. Dowling in the eye.

"How is Marybeth?" Mrs. Dowling asked. "I haven't seen her in a while. That little store and the ranch keeps her busy."

I jerked my head up. I shouldn't be surprised. The whole town probably knew I was visiting Marybeth at her shop, but they didn't know why.

"She's well," I said carefully, not wanting to feed the fire of gossip.

A faint cry came from the rear of the house, where Suzanne and Mrs. Dowling lived.

"It's Annie," Suzanne said by way of apology. She started to stand, but her grandmother laid a hand on her knee.

"I'll get her. You go on and visit some more." Mrs. Dowling set her cup of tea down and rose.

"Gran," Suzanne protested.

"Stay. I'd like to have a moment with my great-granddaughter." Mrs. Dowling's eyes sparkled. Then she looked at me and said, "I imagine Tom might enjoy having grandchildren, even if all he can see is photos of them."

I was pretty sure every ounce of color blanched from my face.

"Don't mind her," Suzanne said as soon as Mrs. Dowling had disappeared through the door. "When she remembers what year it is, she loves to say exactly what she thinks. She doesn't mean anything by it."

I nodded, but I still felt like I should get up and bolt right back to Chicago.

"What is Marybeth up to these days?" Suzanne asked tentatively.

I tensed. Was she about to grill me? We weren't exactly friends when we were younger, but she'd dated a few guys on the football team, so I remembered her pretty well. And I didn't ever think of her as the protective type, ready to pounce on any guy she deemed not worthy of her friend.

"I don't really see much of anyone these days, not since Annie was born," she added. "Talk about a difference from high school." There was a note of sadness in her voice, and I realized her question had nothing at all to do with me.

"She's busy, I think." I paused, deciding not to mention how I'm pretty sure the store isn't doing well. I opted for humor instead. "She made me decorate a Christmas tree."

Suzanne smiled at that. "That sounds like Marybeth. I've worried about her, living out on that ranch alone with Luke."

"Why is that?" The words came out sharply. I racked my brain but I couldn't ever remember a time I thought Luke Noble was a danger to his own sister. But if he was now—

"Oh, not like that!" Suzanne's eyes went wide. "Sorry, I thought you knew, but I guess you don't since you haven't been here."

"Know what?"

She sighed and moved her gaze to the window, where the snow was beginning to fall again. "Luke lost his wife two years ago, right around Christmas. It really did a number on him. Marybeth had moved out after he got married and her parents gave him the ranch and moved to Florida. But then Liz was in that accident and she was so worried about him that she gave up her apartment and moved back to the ranch. He hasn't been easy to live with, but she didn't want to leave him alone. She basically had to run the place for a while. He was angry for a long time, but I think he's mostly just . . . sad now."

My mind flicked back in time. Liz had been Luke's high school girlfriend. They were the golden couple, the one everyone else wished they could be. For obvious reasons, I never got along with Luke, but I felt bad for him, losing the one person he wanted to spend his life with so young.

"What happened to her?" I asked. My curiosity had gotten the better of me.

"Car wreck, up on the interstate. She'd gone shopping in Billings for Christmas. A truck driver fell asleep and sideswiped her car right off the highway."

I couldn't imagine. Losing Mom had been rough, but at least, even at eight years old, I'd known it was coming. It still hollowed me out, but losing her hadn't been a surprise. "That's awful," I murmured.

"It was. Excuse me, there's someone at the desk. Thanks for talking with me, Gabe. It was nice to catch up a little." She gave me a friendly smile before standing to greet her guest.

I stood and headed up the stairs to my room. It made sense now why Marybeth went overboard with the decorations at her shop. Her brother probably couldn't stand them at home. Too many memories, too much pain.

I understood that. If I was honest with myself, it was exactly why I'd avoided everything Christmas since leaving Bent Creek.

And knowing this about Luke—and how Marybeth had taken on the ranch along with her shop to help her brother—stilled something in my soul.

It made me want to give Marybeth the best Christmas of her life.

Chapter Eleven

Marybeth

I stood on my tiptoes, searching for Larkin and Diego among the crowd gathered around the enormous tree set up in the town square. The tree lighting was an annual tradition, dating back to before I was born. Everyone came. There were more people downtown than I'd seen all year.

As I scanned the people who'd gathered, part of me wondered if I wasn't also searching for Gabe.

My eyes finally landed on Larkin, and I walked around the outside of the crowd to get to her.

"Where's Diego?" I asked when I finally reached her.

"Mom wasn't up to coming, so I left him home with her. I kind of worried that I might lose him in all of this." Larkin frowned at the tree. "Maybe I should've brought him, though. He'd love the tree."

"He wouldn't remember it," I said, squeezing her hand. "And you can always bring him next year."

She smiled at me. "Thanks, Marybeth. You always know how to make me feel like I'm doing the right thing."

"You are, especially with Diego." I dropped her hand and let my eyes rove the crowd. Dusk had fallen, and it wouldn't be long before the mayor stood up for her usual speech and the tree was plugged in—with lights from my store.

The town of Bent Creek was always my biggest customer, and this year, they were pretty much keeping me afloat. I admired the tree, and my eyes wandered back to everyone gathered here.

"Looking for Gabe?" Larkin asked, a teasing note to her voice.

"No. Well . . ." I didn't keep secrets from Larkin. "Yes." I sighed. "I don't even know why."

"Uh, because he's still crazy hot and it's clear he likes you and you still have a crush on him?"

My cheeks went warm. She was right about two out of three, as much as I hated to admit that last one.

"I don't know. He didn't come by today. Or yesterday. And he's here to get me to sign away my business. Remember?" I rubbed my gloved hands together, warding away the growing cold.

"Marybeth." Larkin's voice was so serious that I stopped looking and turned to her. She had both hands on her hips. "You literally fell into his arms and he didn't put you down until you asked him to. I bet the chemistry was *sizzling*."

The cold disappeared completely as I remembered that moment. I could have sworn he was going to bend down and kiss me. And the worst part?

I wanted it to happen.

I wanted it so badly that it was all I'd really thought about since then. Every time the door opened at the shop—which wasn't often—I'd hoped it was Gabe. But he'd stayed away, and I didn't know why.

"Maybe it was," I admitted. "But that doesn't take away the fact that he's here to get me to sign that contract. What if he's using me? Pretending to be into me so I'll sign?" I hated it, but I had to be realistic. I wasn't a moony-eyed teenager anymore.

"He might be." Larkin shrugged. "But you won't know unless you go for it and see what happens. What's the worst thing that can happen?"

"He'll break my heart and go back to Chicago. Then the shop fails because I have no customers and I lose it anyway and they swoop in and buy it from the bank. And I have to live with Luke at the ranch for the rest of my life because I have no career and no one wants to be with a failure of a woman."

Larkin blinked at me. "Okay. *So* . . . that won't happen. You know why? Because if the worst happened—and that's a big *if*—anyone in this town will give you a job. Then you and I can get a place together with Diego once I can finally start putting money away."

I ran the toe of my boot over the packed down snow. She was right. I had options . . . they just weren't really the ones I wanted. But I didn't dare say that to my best friend because the last thing I'd want to do is hurt her feelings.

"Oh, look. There's Gabe. Gabe!" Larkin stood on her toes and waved her mittened hand over the crowd.

I bit back a wince. How desperate would he think I was, having my friend yell for him like that?

"Oh, great. Mrs. Young cornered him. You'd better go rescue him before she drags out every secret he has." Larkin put two hands on my back and gave me a gentle shove.

"Larkin!"

"Go!" She waved her hands at me. "He'll thank you."

That was probably true. Mrs. Young spread gossip like wildfire. Nothing was safe around her. I drew in a breath, smoothed my hair, and made my way in the direction Larkin had indicated.

When I found them, Gabe was pressed up against a table filled with candy and crafts for kids. When I caught the desperate look in his eyes, I covered my mouth to hide my laugh.

Thinking quickly, I called out his name. "Gabe!"

He glanced past her toward me, relief coloring his face.

"Gabe!" I moved faster toward him. "I need your help. Hi, Mrs. Young. I'm sorry. I need Gabe right now. It's an emergency." I reached for his arm, gripping the fabric of his coat and pulling him after me—and realizing an emergency would pique Mrs. Young's attention like nothing else.

We had to move fast, or she'd follow us.

I led Gabe through the people, snaking back and forth, and around to the other side of the tree. I didn't stop until I was sure she wasn't behind us.

"What's wrong?" he asked as soon as I stopped.

"Nothing." I realized I was still holding his sleeve and pulled my hand away, hoping he hadn't noticed. "Larkin thought I should rescue you from Mrs. Young before she got you to confess to every misdeed you've ever done."

"Thanks." He ran his hand over his coat sleeve. He'd definitely noticed how long I'd held onto it. "Wait. Just how much trouble do you think I get up to?"

I shrugged and looked around to hide a smile as I remembered him complaining that I'd called him a villain.

"Are you looking for your brothers? I can leave if you need me to."

My gaze shot back to him. He looked genuinely concerned for me, and my heart melted even more than it already had upon seeing him again. "No need to worry about that. The only one still here is Luke."

"And he wouldn't be here," Gabe finished for me.

"Right." I paused. "How did you know that?"

"Suzanne Dowling mentioned it."

I nodded. Suzanne had always been a good friend, but I hadn't seen much of her since her daughter was born. I was busy with the shop, the ranch, and helping Larkin, but I really should've made the time to visit Suzanne. I made a mental note to ensure that happened.

"I'm sorry about that. For Luke, I mean." His face was drawn into a serious expression, and the carefully held together pieces of my heart threatened to burst.

"Thanks. It's been tough." I didn't dare say more. Watching Luke suffer was the hardest thing I'd ever done in my life. Mom was so worried after Liz's funeral that she called every day from Florida. Dad asked if I'd take over the ranch.

I did, for a while. I did everything and held my shop and Luke together too.

"You're a good person, Marybeth," Gabe said. "It sounds like you gave up a lot."

I didn't know if it was the way he'd said it or just hearing someone finally acknowledge everything I'd set aside to help my brother, but that dam I'd built inside me to keep it all in, to stay strong, to keep my shop going among everything else finally burst open.

Tears stung the corners of my eyes, and I crossed my arms and looked away. Everyone's attention had turned to the mayor, who was standing at the podium to begin her speech.

"Hey." Gabe lifted a hand. He hesitated for a second and then pulled off his glove and wiped away the first tears that started to fall. "It's all right. You're all right."

I shook my head. He didn't know how close I was to losing the shop. Just a couple more bad months, and I was going to have problems. And I didn't dare tell him, knowing what he was after.

But he wiped away another tear, and I closed my eyes. The warmth of his hand, the kindness, the sheer intimacy of it . . . it overcame my emotions about Luke and Bent Creek Christmas and the entire course of my life. I gulped a sob and opened my eyes.

Gabe was still there. And he was watching me with a curious tenderness I'd never seen before.

He reached for my hand. I didn't think twice about his motives—I couldn't do that right now.

I just wanted someone to hold my hand.

So I dropped my arms, and I let him wrap his hand around mine. And together we stood and watched as the lights flickered to life on the tree.

Afterward, he didn't say a word, but he held my hand as he walked me to my car. I paused by the door, and he let go. He watched me for a moment, and I waited for him to say something. When he didn't, I gave him a tentative smile as I gestured to the people streaming down the street under the glow of the streetlights and the twinkling Christmas lights the town strung up around the lampposts.

"Don't you miss all of this?" I asked.

He took a moment, looking out at the people, the shops, the town we've known since the day we were born.

"Maybe a little," he said, turning back to me. "The way it was before. But that's gone now."

I bit my lip, studying the blue of his eyes, the way his nose curved, the hard line of his chin. "It's not. It's still here, if you want it."

He didn't say anything, but he lifted his hand to my face and cupped my cheek. My heart thudded and images of him kissing me right up against my trusty old Honda flipped through my mind.

But he gave me a sad smile instead. "I don't know. But maybe I'll find out. Good night, Marybeth."

"Good night," I whispered as he dropped his hand and strode away in the snow.

Chapter Twelve

Gabe

There were three texts and one missed call from Chicago when I finally looked at my phone last night. All but one were from Hatfield. The last text was from Mr. Durnstorff himself, threatening to send Hatfield down here to finish the job.

I felt sick looking at them. If I didn't get Marybeth to sign that contract, I'd lose my job. But if I got her to sign . . .

Looking at the texts again the next day, I rubbed my hands over my face. What was wrong with me? When I left Bent Creek, I wouldn't have cared if the entire town got swallowed up in a sinkhole. But now?

In between thinking about how soft Marybeth's skin had felt beneath my hand, I was imagining grabbing a beer at the Pine Street Bar with my brother Nick or fishing in summer with Jackson. Wondering how the ranch would look if I could just get my hands on it. And replaying Marybeth's words in my mind . . . *It's still here if you want it.*

Was it? Could Bent Creek put the past to rest and welcome a Harker back to town?

It was crazy to even contemplate, but I thought about it when I walked into town earlier. The looks I got from people I passed felt friendlier. I stopped and petted Christa Appleby's dog, and Mrs. Foley asked me how I liked her cookies. I acted as if I hadn't left them in Marybeth's shop the day I'd run out after catching her fall.

And then I'd found myself in the real estate office, talking with Kyle Clemmons, who'd been a sophomore on the football team when I was a senior. He'd done some research for other clients interested in our ranch and told me that all he knew was that the property belonged to a company called Chestnut Moon, LLC. All calls, emails, and letters to them about buying the property had gone unanswered.

I'd walked in that door with a raging curiosity—and left fully intending to get my hands on that property. What I'd do with it if I got it, I didn't know.

I'd think about that later.

Back at the B&B, I found two more voicemails from the firm. I knew I should listen to them, reassure Hatfield and Mr. Durnstorff that I had this all under control. But the truth was, I didn't. And I wasn't sure I wanted to. So I ignored them and spent the afternoon walking the ranch property instead.

In my head, the place was mine, even though I absolutely knew I was trespassing. If I could get a hold of that company, what would they ask for a place like this? I had money in the bank and assets I could liquidate. Durnstorff and Vibert had been good to me over the years. I felt a twinge of guilt at ignoring the calls, but that faded the more I walked.

I passed the old tree that had once held a tire swing, the frozen pond, broken fences that had once held more cattle than I could count as a kid. Every corner I turned, another memory came back—both good and bad.

Yet the good far outweighed the bad. And I missed my family.

Eventually, the sun began to sink lower over the mountains in the west, and I headed back to the B&B. I found Suzanne, baby Annie, and Mrs. Dowling all dressed up and about to walk out the door.

"You all look very nice tonight. Is there a show in town?" I asked as I held the door open for them.

"It's the Holiday Hope Dance," Suzanne said, tilting her head. "You didn't forget that?"

"Right," I said, pretending like I knew all along that it was tonight. "Lots of good memories there."

"For sure," Suzanne replied. "Aren't you going?"

"I . . . uh . . . I don't know. I have some work to do."

Mrs. Dowling shook her head, as if she pitied me, and I wondered if she knew it was me or if she thought I was Pops again.

They left, and I stood there in the entryway. Should I go? It would be a lot of people in one place. But so was the tree lighting, and I went to that. No one seemed bothered by me being there. Just like no one seemed to mind me walking around town today.

Marybeth might be there.

What I'd give to feel her hand in mine again, to brush my fingers over her cheek, to hold her close and show her exactly how I felt about her. Which was . . . what exactly?

I didn't know, but I wanted to find out.

I took the stairs two at a time and emerged a half hour later, freshly showered and wearing the nicest pair of jeans I owned with a button-down black shirt. I hadn't been gone from Bent Creek so long that I'd forgotten no one wears a suit to the Holiday Hope Dance.

When I arrived at the community center, the dance was in full swing. The place was a mess of Christmas, and unlike the first time I stepped into Marybeth's shop, it didn't bother me. In fact, it felt almost like home.

Smiling at the warmth buzzing through me and eager to lay eyes on Marybeth, I paid a couple of high school kids manning the door and scanned the packed room. "Jingle Bell Rock" was in full swing from a band at the far end of the room, and the dance floor was packed.

I skirted around the outside of it, waving to Larkin and nodding to Kyle, the real estate agent I'd spoken with earlier. Then I spotted her. She wore a shimmering red top that swished around a pair of dark-washed jeans tucked into brown cowboy boots. I lifted my hand to wave—and stopped.

She was smiling as she danced—right at some guy I couldn't recognize from here.

How could I have been so dense? Of course she was seeing someone—she was too beautiful, too kind, too incredible not to. But then why had she let me take her hand?

I scowled at the two of them. I could have walked away. I *should* have walked away.

But I didn't.

Instead, I strode toward them as fast as I could.

Chapter Thirteen

Marybeth

"Is that Gabe Creason?" Ben Collins asked as I was still laughing at his impression of our fourth grade teacher.

My laugh choked in my throat as I followed his gaze.

Gabe was walking quickly toward us with a determined look on his face. But when he saw me watching him, he stopped. Determination slipped away to panic, and just before he turned away, I thought I saw embarrassment. He disappeared as fast as he'd appeared.

"Excuse me, Ben," I said, lifting my hair off my neck.

He waved, and I walked as quickly as I could in the same direction Gabe had gone. I was sure Ben knew Gabe had walked me to my car at the tree lighting. The whole town probably knew. But I didn't really care about gossip at that moment.

I only cared about what Gabe thought.

I found him by the Ladies' Auxiliary VFW table, studying frosted cupcakes as if they were the most interesting thing in the room.

"Gabe?" I stood off to the side, mostly because the two women collecting payment for the snacks and drinks at the table were two of my mom's closest friends. They'd probably be calling her first thing in the morning, if they hadn't already, to tell her who her daughter had been talking and dancing with at the Holiday Hope Dance.

He looked up at me and Mrs. Adams and Mrs. Garcia's eyes followed his. He glanced quickly at them, pulled out a few bills from his wallet, and took two cups of punch from the table.

He handed one to me, and I drank it in just a few gulps. I hadn't realized how thirsty I'd been. "Thank you."

He nodded, but said nothing as he held out his hand for my cup. I waited while he tossed the cups into the nearest trash can.

"Ben is an old friend," I blurted out the second he returned.

Gabe lifted his eyebrows. "All right."

"I just . . . I wanted you to know that." I twisted my hands together. Had I imagined the look of jealousy on his face when he was walking toward us? Maybe I had. But I'd thought that after last night—

"Then I suppose you wouldn't mind dancing with me then?" Gabe held out a hand.

I couldn't keep the grin from my face as I placed my hand in his.

He led me to the dance floor. A hundred eyes were on us, but I didn't care. Let them talk. I'd deal with the fallout from my brother tomorrow. Tonight, all I wanted was to feel alive.

And Gabe made me feel more than alive. He made me feel as if I was *living*.

As the band began playing the opening strands of "I'll Be Home for Christmas," Gabe wrapped his arms around me. I slowly melded into him, letting my own arms circle his waist.

I leaned my head back to look up at him. He looked lost in thought for a moment and then he turned his gaze down toward me.

"This song played at this same dance my senior year." His voice was low, the words meant only for my ears.

"I remember." Of course I remembered. I'd never forget that dance, the last one I'd seen him at. A few weeks later, his stepdad would be arrested, and his world turned upside down. But at that dance, he'd been the Gabe I'd fallen in love with two years before. Strong, quiet but friendly, so handsome it was hard to pull my eyes away from him. He'd looked at me once that evening, studied me for several long agonizing minutes, and I'd thought he'd finally *seen* me. But then he'd turned away, back to his friends, and I'd tucked my hope away yet again.

"You wore a gold dress. It was very shiny." He laughed just a little, and I smiled in surprise.

"You remember that?" I'd loved that dress. "Larkin told me I'd blind everyone with that gold."

"You blinded me, but it wasn't because of the dress."

I didn't know what to say to that. I'd thought he'd never noticed me back then.

But he had.

He shifted his hands on my back, pulling me closer, and I rested the side of my head on his chest. The black button-down he wore was soft, and I closed my eyes as his closeness warmed my skin. His heart beat against my ear, and I imagined mine beating in sync.

I never wanted this song to end.

But it did, of course. He pulled away, and I reluctantly lifted my head. We danced to the next two faster songs, and by then I desperately needed something more to drink.

Gabe grabbed water this time, and we stood near the big Christmas tree in the corner, drinking it and watching everyone else dance.

"Did you decorate this one?" He gestured at the tree, which had a fun Western theme.

"No, but most of it came from my store. The town of Bent Creek is my biggest customer." I didn't mean to sound bitter when I said that—because I was thankful for them, after all—but it came out that way anyway.

He watched me, and reality crept into my mind, pushing away the moment we'd just shared on the dance floor. Would he use my worries about the shop to tell me why I should agree to that deal from his company?

But he said nothing. Instead, he plucked one of the cowboy hats from the tree and held it out. "I don't remember seeing these in Bent Creek Christmas."

"That's because I don't carry hats, only Christmas decorations. I mean, I suppose I *could* stock hats, but they'd probably need lights attached or reindeer antlers or something festive."

He grimaced, and I laughed. "Would someone actually buy that?" he asked.

"I don't know." I took the hat from his hand and studied it. "But I think this might look better here . . ." I stood on my tiptoes and set it on his head.

He didn't protest, so I set my water bottle down and adjusted it until it sat at just the right angle. By some miracle, it actually fit him. I stepped back to study my handiwork.

"Now there's the Gabe Creason I know." My voice came out in a whisper as a hundred different memories chased themselves through my mind.

Slowly, Gabe set his water bottle down next to mine, his eyes never leaving me. Then he reached for my hand. My heart ratcheted up as his fingers closed around mine, and before I knew it, he was pulling me behind the tree.

Strains of "The Christmas Song" filtered in from the dance floor as he pulled me closer. We were only partially hidden back here. Plenty of people stood off to the side of the tree, talking and watching the dancing, but whether they were looking back here, I didn't know.

I didn't really care either.

All I cared about was the way Gabe was watching me with those startling eyes. I couldn't have moved if I'd wanted to. Just the way he looked at me took my breath away, and I clung to his shirt as he lifted a hand to caress my face.

My breath caught in my throat, and I closed my eyes at his touch.

"Marybeth." His voice was jagged and husky as he said my name.

I couldn't seem to drag up any real sound at all, only a sigh as I leaned against him. I opened my eyes just enough to see his go dark, and then his mouth was on mine.

I gripped his shirt like a drowning woman as his lips parted. I clung to him like I could never get enough. How long had I wished for this to happen? How many nights had I dreamed of a scenario just like this?

Everything that had gone wrong in my life flashed away the second Gabe's lips met mine. Nothing mattered except him, me, and this tiny slice of time.

He groaned as he lifted a hand to the back of my head, and I thrilled in the knowledge that he wanted me as much as I wanted him.

He drove the kiss even deeper, and I was lost completely. We were on a dangerous edge, and my brother's words echoed somewhere in the back of my mind.

But if this was danger, then I wanted it—I *needed* it—in my life.

And I wouldn't let anything else get in the way.

Chapter Fourteen

Marybeth

Christmas Eve dawned brightly, the sun's rays illuminating the snow and making it impossible to feel anything but happy.

Or maybe that was just me, reliving that kiss behind the Christmas tree yet again.

I'd opened the shop for a few hours in the morning, in the desperate hope that someone might need cookie ingredients or a last minute present. But so far, my only customers had been Larkin and Diego, who had come to exchange gifts.

I'd snuck out of the house while Luke was out feeding the horses this morning, not wanting to know if anyone had texted him about seeing me and Gabe together last night. He would find out at some point, and it would be a matter of me deciding whether to mention it before that happened.

But how could I even broach that subject with Luke? I was so careful around him. The grief would never go away, but at least he could function now. If he found out about me and Gabe . . . I was so afraid that would set him back. And I wasn't sure *I* could go back to those dark days when I carried everything on my shoulders. I had enough to carry now as it was.

I straightened up behind the counter. It was Christmas Eve. I didn't have any customers, but I had peppermint hot chocolate, a lightly falling snow outside, and all the Christmas cheer possible inside my shop. I poured myself a hot chocolate and determined to focus only on good things for the rest of the day.

Which meant, of course, that I kept sneaking glances at the door to see if Gabe might show up. He'd plugged his number into my phone last night after the dance, but I didn't dare text him. Not yet.

Just as I was straightening the ribbons on one of the trees near the window and remembering again how it felt when Gabe said my name as if I was the only thing that mattered to him, Luke arrived.

My brother *never* came into Bent Creek Christmas. He barely tolerated the small, simple tree I'd put up at home. But he was here now, complete with a scowl that could scare small children.

And I knew exactly why.

"Luke—" I started as I moved toward him, but he cut me off immediately.

"Have you lost your mind?" He strode across the store until he was right in front of me. "Because I can't think of another reason why I'd hear that you were all over Gabe Creason at the dance last night."

I winced. I hadn't been *all over* Gabe, but when I thought about how intense that kiss had gotten, I realized that maybe I had been. It had been a huge risk, and now I was going to pay for it.

"It wasn't . . ." I fumbled for the right words. "I didn't . . . Luke, you—"

Luke's face darkened as he interrupted me again. "Did he force you? You don't have to explain it. Just tell me he did, and I swear you'll never have to see his face again."

My eyes widened. "No!" I didn't want to know what he meant by that last part. "Please, just listen to me. He didn't . . . I mean . . . I kissed him, okay? If you're going to be mad at someone, be mad at me." It wasn't the truth, but if Gabe hadn't kissed me last night, I probably would have taken things into my own hands. And if it kept Luke's anger focused on me and not Gabe, I'd say anything.

His eyes went cold. "*Why*?"

I crossed my arms. "I'm a grown woman, Luke. I can make my own decisions."

He regarded me like something he'd never seen before. "You're messing with a lot of history, Marybeth. With things you don't understand."

I blew out an irritated breath. "I understand well enough to know it's all in the past. It was between Dad and Mr. Harker, and that's over now. Don't you want to move on?"

"That's impossible." His voice was flat. "End it now, Marybeth."

I gaped at him. What right did he think he had to order me around? Especially after I took care of him—of *everything*—for a solid year and then some.

"He'll break your heart. And you'll find yourself in a mess you can't get out of."

"You're living in the past. And I'll see who I want to see. I don't need you acting like Dad."

His nostrils flared, and then he turned around and stalked out of the store.

I stepped backward until I hit the counter. I was shaking, and I wasn't sure if it was from anger or from the fear of seeing Luke so anchored in what had happened years ago. Collapsing against the sturdy wood, I drew in a shuddering breath.

I was worried about Luke. He needed peace, hard work, and routine. He needed to keep healing. If this thing with Gabe was actually going somewhere, I'd have to convince Luke that things had changed. That it would be all right. That *I* would be okay. That Gabe was a good man.

Was he? I thought so. But there was that lingering elephant in the room—the sales contract he'd come here to get me to sign. The next time I saw him, I'd bring it up again. And he would have to decide what happened next, because I wasn't going to sell.

Ever.

The door opened again, and I stood up as a man and woman in expensive wool coats entered. Customers! Actual, paying customers would be the perfect way to close the store today. And then maybe I could talk to Gabe and then figure out a way to soothe Luke's unfounded fears.

The woman was casting her eyes around the shop. But instead of glancing at things one by one and admiring the various sorts of decorations and gift items, she seemed to be looking at everything more shrewdly.

While the man was staring right at me.

I smiled at him, wanting them to feel welcome. "Merry Christmas! Welcome to Bent Creek. Let me know if I can help you find anything, and please feel free to have a cup of peppermint hot chocolate while you look around." I gestured at the Crock Pot on the counter.

The man's eyes flickered toward the hot chocolate and then back to me. "Are you Marybeth Noble?"

I hesitated. There was something oddly direct about the question. "I am," I said as cheerfully as I could.

"Colin Hatfield, with the firm of Durnstorff and Vibert." He whipped out a folio that was identical to the one Gabe had brought. "We've increased our offer to buy this building."

I stared down at the papers he held out in front of me without actually seeing them. Then I raised my head to look Mr. Hatfield in the eye. "You work with Gabe?" I couldn't imagine him going into an office with these two every day.

"Yes. He's no longer on this project. I received word that he arrived back in Chicago this morning. We'd like to wrap this up today, Ms. Noble." He shook the folio just a little and held out a pen.

My eyes drifted down to the pen, but I didn't see it. Gabe was gone?

A coldness traced through my veins, turning my happy memories of the night before into dust.

He'd left without a word.

I pressed a hand to my stomach, trying hard to keep my expression neutral even as my world fell apart. He *was* using me . . .

Luke was right. Gabe broke my heart.

I thought I would be sick. I turned away and pressed my other hand over my mouth, squeezing my eyes shut to force the tears away. I couldn't cry in front of these people. I *wouldn't*.

"Ms. Noble? If you have concerns, I can go through this contract with you," Mr. Hatfield said from behind me.

I dragged in a breath and forced it out. I could *not* think about Gabe right now. I could fall apart later, when I was alone. But at this moment, I needed to let these people know in no uncertain terms that I wasn't going to sell.

"There's no need for that," I said as I turned around. "I'm not interested. Now, I need to close up, so if you aren't interested in making a purchase, I have to ask you to leave."

They glanced at each other, and this time the woman spoke. "I had an interesting call with a Joseph Caldwell yesterday, Miss Noble. Are you familiar with him?"

I nodded. He was Mrs. Caldwell's son. He'd moved to California years ago to pursue a tech career, long before his mother passed away and willed me this building.

"Did you know he knew nothing about this building? He claims he never saw the will that left it to you."

My stomach lurched. This wasn't good. "I asked the lawyer about that when I found out she'd left it to me. He said she'd left it to me in appreciation for visiting and taking her on errands. The lawyer insisted the will was all valid and normal."

"Apparently it wasn't. Mr. Caldwell is *very* interested in reopening the estate. We have some lawyers who could help him with it if . . . well . . ." She looked at Mr. Hatfield.

"But I'm sure they'd be too busy to do that if we have them tied up with the transfer of this property to our company. Don't you think so, Gwen?"

The woman named Gwen nodded, and I clenched my hands to my sides.

"Think about it, Ms. Noble," Mr. Hatfield said as he closed the folio with the contract. "You could give yourself a nice little Christmas present with this money."

"We'll need an answer in two days," his colleague added.

I said nothing as they found their way to the door. The second it closed behind them, I grabbed my stuff and locked up.

Once in the Honda, I blasted the heat and headed to the B&B.

Because I refused to believe Gabe was gone without evidence.

Chapter Fifteen

Gabe

It was late when the plane landed in Billings. I had a two hour drive ahead of me, but even after nearly an entire day on planes with a few hours spent in Chicago in between, I wasn't tired.

I couldn't wait to see Marybeth.

The Christmas Eve night highway was nearly empty, and I pushed the rental as far over the speed limit as I dared. All I wanted was to get back to Bent Creek, find Marybeth, and tell her my news.

I'd quit my job.

I smiled at the black landscape ahead of me, cut only by the beams of my headlights. The second I'd landed, I'd wasted no time in getting to the office. There were people there, just as I'd expected. Greed doesn't take a holiday.

I cleaned out the few personal items in my office, then I found someone in human resources and submitted my resignation. I stopped by Hatfield's office, only to discover he'd come to Bent Creek with another of the bosses, Gwen Rowe.

My texts and calls to both of them had gone unanswered. Turnabout was fair play, I supposed.

But they'd only find themselves disappointed. Marybeth wouldn't sell to them either.

The only thing I could do was go back and find them in person. It wasn't until after I'd paid a quick visit to my apartment, ran to the bank, hopped a cab back to the airport, and was in the air that I realized they'd probably come armed with more than just the promise of money.

I could've smacked myself on the forehead for not thinking of that sooner. If I had, I would've warned Marybeth. What dirt had they dug up? I'd spent the entire rest of the flight worrying about it, and the second I stepped off, I sent a text to Marybeth.

Of course it was late. And it was Christmas Eve. She hadn't replied.

I sped through the darkness until finally I reached Bent Creek. I rolled past the B&B, where I'd given up my room. I hadn't expected to be back in town tonight. I thought I'd be in Chicago for at least a couple of days to get this business taken care of.

There were only two options now: spend the night in my truck, or find Marybeth.

I swallowed the old fear of paying a visit to the Nobles' ranch at nearly midnight and aimed the truck in that direction.

The past was the past, and if Luke Noble didn't like it, he'd need to get over that soon.

And I hoped *soon* was now.

Because the second I stepped out of the truck, I found him on the front porch, aiming a rifle at me.

Chapter Sixteen

Marybeth

Sleep was something that wouldn't come, so when Gabe returned, I was sitting cross-legged on the living room couch across from our sad tree. To distract myself from thoughts of Gabe disappearing from the B&B without a word to me and those people who'd visited my shop with their threats, I'd made some hot chocolate and pulled an old photo album from the bookshelf.

Glancing through images of my brothers, myself, and our parents in happier times brought a smile to my face. I missed the rest of my family something awful.

Would we ever spend another Christmas together?

I'd swiped away a tear and just turned another page when Luke came galloping down the stairs. He'd thrown on a wrinkled t-shirt with a pair of jeans, and his boots were untied as he grabbed the hunting rifle from the wall and slammed through the front door.

I glanced at the clock. It was past midnight. Officially Christmas. He must have heard a bear.

But then I heard the snow and gravel crunching under tires. That was no bear.

I set the photo album aside and yanked my coat out of the closet. Wrapping it around myself, I followed Luke outside in my slippers.

And found him aiming that rifle at Gabe.

My heart fell to my feet. The numbing cold disappeared, and all I could think was that *he'd come back*.

I threw a hand over my mouth as I squinted through the darkness and the swiftly falling snow. The door to Gabe's truck was still open, spilling light into a small circle nearby. Gabe stood there with his hands raised.

I swallowed hard, my disappointment from earlier shriveling up in the face of hope.

He was wearing the hat. The cheap one from the dance that I'd taken off the tree and set on his head. That hope blossomed even more inside me. He was *here*!

"Luke!" I hissed, finding my voice. "What are you doing? Put that down."

He ignored me, keeping his eyes on Gabe. "Get the hell off my property."

My muscles tightened. Luke's face was unreadable. Out by the truck, Gabe didn't move.

"It's Christmas," Gabe said, like that might change Luke's mind. "I'm only here to talk to Marybeth." His gaze flickered toward me.

That was possibly the worst thing he could have said. Why did he think coming here would be okay? Why didn't he just text me?

Or had he? My phone had been plugged into the charger since I'd gotten home.

"Are you deaf, Creason?" Luke called out through the snow and the darkness.

Out of the corner of my eye, light streamed from the door of the bunkhouse. A few of the men who lived on the ranch stepped outside.

This wasn't going to end well. And if Luke wouldn't act reasonably, then I was the only one who could stop it.

Without even a glance back at my brother, I crossed to the edge of the porch and ran down the steps.

"Marybeth?" Luke sounded more confused than angry, but I didn't look back.

I flinched as snow fell over the tops of my slippers. Even as it began to soak through, I didn't stop. Not until I reached Gabe.

He'd lowered his hands as he watched me make my way toward him. His coat was open and his normally smooth jaw was unshaven and all I wanted to do was throw myself at him.

"Are you crazy?" Luke called from the porch. "Get out of the snow!"

I stopped in front of Gabe and turned around to face my brother. "I'm not the one aiming a gun at someone who's done nothing at all! *You're* the crazy one, Luke, and I'm not moving until you put that rifle down."

Luke stared at me like he'd never seen me before. Then he glanced at Gabe, let out a string of swears that would have made our mother clock him on the back of the head, and then—finally—he lowered the rifle.

I glanced at the men by the bunkhouse. Luke took the hint and motioned at them to go back inside.

I fixed my gaze on Luke. "Now will you give us a minute?"

He hesitated.

I glanced at Gabe's rental. "I guess I'll get in the truck and we can go—"

"Fine." Luke practically spat the word. "But you—" He pointed at Gabe. "Stay outside. I'll be in the living room."

Probably staring daggers at us through the door. But I didn't care. Because Gabe was here.

Luke lingered on the porch until I'd picked my way through the snow. The truck door shut behind me, and I heard Gabe's boots crunching down the same path I'd taken.

Back on the porch, I fixed Luke with a look until he finally went back inside. The porch swing was blessedly clear of snow, and Gabe pointed at it.

"Sit. And take off those slippers before you get frostbite." He slid his arms from his coat, and as soon as I'd done what he'd said, he knelt down and wrapped my numb feet in his coat.

I bit my lip. It was the gentlest, kindest thing anyone had ever done for me.

He sat next to me, close but not touching.

I wrapped my arms around myself. "I thought you'd gone for good."

"Marybeth, I'm sorry." Those blue eyes found mine, and I saw the emotion reflected in them. "I should have at least texted you before I left. After the dance, I knew I had to do something. That . . ." He closed his eyes a second before opening them again. "That kiss clarified a lot for me. I needed to get back to Chicago as fast as possible."

"What did it clarify?" My voice came out in a whisper and my fingers dug into the sides of my arms.

"I hated my job. And I have for a while, but being here . . ." He sighed and glanced out over the darkened land before his gaze landed back on mine. "It was a lot of things that finally brought that home for me. The town didn't react the way I'd assumed it would. The ranch .

. ." He swallowed, and my heart broke thinking about the state of the Harker Ranch. "You."

"And maybe Christmas?" I said with a tiny smile.

He laughed quietly. "Maybe a little. But mostly . . ." He didn't finish, but his eyes swept my face.

I warmed at the attention, but I couldn't let myself get carried away. I glanced down at the floor of the porch, where my feet were coming back to life in pins and needles inside Gabe's coat.

"I thought you'd used me. And when you couldn't get what you wanted, you left and sent those other people to finish the job." It hurt saying it out loud, but no more than it had hurt me to learn about it earlier that day.

"Marybeth." Gabe laid a hand on my leg.

I stilled. Then I looked up at him, and the concern that lined his face and made his eyes go dark made me pinch my lips together. "But you didn't, did you?"

He shook his head. "I didn't know they'd come until I got back to Chicago. I'm sorry. If I'd known, I would have waited."

I closed my eyes. My hand found his, and he wrapped his fingers around mine.

"What did they say?" he asked.

I told him about Mrs. Caldwell's son. About the will. About how I feared I had no way out of this.

"There's a way." He set a finger under my chin and turned my head until I was looking him in the eyes. "It's part of why I went back to Chicago. Tomorrow we'll pay them a visit, and they'll head back to the city for good."

I blinked at him. "Are you serious?"

He nodded. "Trust me, Marybeth. I have it all figured out."

And I did trust him. Then I did what I'd wanted to do the second I saw him in the driveway.

I threw my arms around his neck and kissed him until every doubt of the past twenty-four hours had disappeared into the stars above us.

Chapter Seventeen

Gabe

"He's either shot out my tires or broken the windows. Probably both."

Marybeth shook her head as she presented me with a heaping helping of egg casserole and a pile of bacon. "He wouldn't. Definitely not the tires, because then you couldn't leave. But the windows . . ."

She screwed up her lips in a way that made me want to forget all about Christmas morning breakfast and spend the next hour kissing her instead.

Except that would be the moment her brother would walk in, and I wasn't sure I was ready for that this early in the morning. Thankfully, he'd given up last night and gone to bed by the time we came inside. Marybeth insisted I stay in the guest room—where I locked the door in case Luke looked outside and saw the truck still parked in his driveway. If it hadn't been ten degrees out, I would have opted to sleep in the truck.

"The truck is fine," Marybeth said, peeking out the window as she poured herself more coffee. "And it's stopped snowing. Maybe we can get out of here before Luke comes back from the stables. I won't be able to corner him long enough to make him exchange gifts until tonight anyway."

With that thought in mind, I started shoveling casserole into my mouth. I closed my eyes at the taste. It reminded me of home. Marybeth joined me at the table, and we were quiet for several minutes while we ate.

"So what exactly is the plan?" she asked after I'd cleared my plate.

I sat back, trying not to think of a second helping. "Since it's Christmas, I'm sure we'll find them at the B&B."

"And then?" Marybeth leaned over her plate in curiosity.

"I'm giving them a check," I said carefully.

"A check." She tilted her head. "What for?"

I wasn't sure how she'd take this, so I wanted to tread carefully. "Enough money to draw their interest to a piece of land outside of town, and away from your building."

She scrunched up her eyebrows. "So it's a sort of deal, right? They only get the money if they use it to buy this other property instead?"

I nodded.

"I don't understand. Why wouldn't they go after that land instead? Why pay them?"

"It's a larger piece of property. More expensive. I just need to convince them that it's a much better investment than a lot in town. Which shouldn't be too hard, since it's easier to get to from both the highway and the resorts."

"But they don't get Bent Creek," she said slowly. "Isn't that what they wanted? The town?"

I pressed my lips together. "They'll come back. It's inevitable. But this will distract them for a while. Long enough for all of us to make some kind of plan."

She tilted her head. "And why are you so sure they'll jump on this offer?"

"Because Hatfield's angry at me, and he likes his revenge." *Please don't ask where the money came from.*

She paused. "Where did this money come from?"

I sighed, then, needing to move, I stood and gathered our plates. "It's mine."

"Gabe." Her voice held a note of disapproval.

I turned on the water in the sink. "I earned it from giving my soul to that place for years, and now I'm finally putting it to good use. If Hatfield knows this is hurting me directly, he'll be more apt to take it."

"I can't let you do that." She appeared next to me, her face troubled.

I shut off the water and turned to face her. "It's not up to you. It's my money and my decision. And this is what I'd like to do with it."

She chewed on her lower lip, and I lifted a hand to her shoulder. "I don't like it," she said as I drew her toward me.

"You don't have to. But it makes me happy to do this. And once they've gone back to Chicago, you can concentrate on growing your business."

She tilted her chin up as my hand found its way around the back of her neck. "But how are you going to buy your ranch?" I'd told her about the decision I'd made before I left for Chicago the day before.

The Harker Ranch would belong to the Harkers again, if it was the last thing I did.

I threaded my fingers through her hair, reveling in how soft it was. "I'll figure it out. I've got some other assets and a few ideas."

She lifted her eyebrows as if she didn't believe me.

"Didn't you tell me there was something about this town?"

She nodded, the corners of her mouth lifting a bit.

I shrugged my shoulders. "It'll work out. One way or the other. And I'm stubborn enough to make it happen. Because you're right. There *is* something about this town, and I believe I'm meant to be here. And I believe your shop is meant to thrive."

Marybeth smiled for real then. "Merry Christmas, Gabe." She stood on her tiptoes and brushed her lips across mine.

"Merry Christmas," I whispered back before pulling her closer to crush her lips against mine.

She sighed against me, and I vowed to erase any doubts from her mind. Her store would succeed. The tourists would come back to Bent Creek. I'd get my ranch.

The work I had to do swirled across my mind as I slowly lost myself in Marybeth. Luke didn't trust me—at all. I couldn't remember the last time I'd talked to my brothers. I had no idea who owned the ranch. And I had no money.

But I had Marybeth, and right now, she was all I needed.

Epilogue

Nick Harker

February

I knew I was home when the snow drifts grew taller than the truck.

Welcome to Montana, the sign said. Home of the people who'd sent my father to prison, the land that no longer belonged to my family, every broken dream I ever had, and the girl I'd left without a word nearly eleven years ago.

Only one thing could get me to come back here, and that was a phone call from my brother.

Gabe had started by rambling on about some business opportunity. I was half tuning out, staring out at the much less bleak Texas landscape, when he'd said the word *ranch*.

That got my attention.

And when I asked him about it, he confirmed exactly what I'd guessed—he wanted to buy back the family ranch.

I shook my head as he talked. My stepbrother was always a dreamer, and here he was, trying to reclaim the past. "It's a bad idea," I'd told him. "A bad investment."

Maybe it was, maybe it wasn't. But it would've meant we had to come back here, and I *never* wanted to come back.

"I'm already here," he said, like he'd read my mind.

I pinched the bridge of my nose. Why he'd put himself through Bent Creek again was beyond me. "Another bad idea."

"I don't know . . ." He sounded amused, and I scowled at the window. "I met someone."

"You're in Bent Creek because of a girl? Who?" No one in their right mind moved to a small mountain town with nothing to offer but a cutesy downtown and no industry to speak of beyond ranching. Which meant this girl had to be someone we knew.

He paused, and I started to grow suspicious. "Gabe?"

"It's Marybeth," he said quickly. "Remember her?"

I said nothing. Then finally, I ground the words out from between my teeth. "Marybeth Noble?"

He made a noncommittal sound.

"Have you got a death wish? Does her father know?" I couldn't imagine old man Noble being all right with that.

"He lives in Florida now. The ranch belongs to Luke."

I laughed, but there was nothing funny about this. "Well, tell her to invite me to your funeral when he kills you."

"We're . . . uh . . . working that out."

I rubbed my hand over my face. Why couldn't Gabe just leave well enough alone? He had to go back there and stir up a hornet's nest. "You better work it out fast. Better yet, call it off. Weren't you in Chicago? Why don't you go back there?"

"Because I'm intending to buy the ranch—*our* ranch. And I need your help. I want us all to go in on it. Together."

I shook my head. "I've gotta go. I'll talk to you later."

But I didn't. Instead, I packed a bag, begged off a leave of absence from the ranch where I'd just been hired on, and drove north.

Not to help Gabe, but to save his life.

He had no idea what he was getting into, and I wasn't about to let him die over it.

Now if only I could get this done without running into Larkin, I'd be done and back to Texas before anyone knew I was in town.

Thank you so much for reading! I hope you enjoyed Gabe and Marybeth's story—and meeting the Harker and Noble families. **Find out what happens next** when Nick comes back to town and sees Larkin, the girl he left nearly eleven years ago, in *A Second Chance in Bent Creek*.

Come home to Bent Creek . . . a small town in Montana where everyone knows everyone, secrets live in the shadows of the mountains, and love is waiting to be found. The Harker Brothers Ranch series tells the stories of six brothers—Gabe, Nick, Jackson, Ward, Colt, and Maverick—as they return with one goal: to get the family ranch back in their hands. Reckoning with their family's past, the Nobles, and each other, each one finds love and home again in their hometown.

Join my email newsletter at catiecahill.com to keep up with everything Bent Creek.

More by Catie Cahill

Visit catiecahill.com for a full list of Catie's books.

About Catie

Catie lives with her family in Kentucky but half her heart is in the Rocky Mountains. Catie loves animals, planning travels, reading, and spending time with her family. Visit her online at catiecahill.com.

www.ingramcontent.com/pod-product-compliance
Lightning Source LLC
Chambersburg PA
CBHW020049310726
48970CB00007B/2476